For
wil

2011

# DREAM
# SOUNDERS

*Carroll Rinehart*

PublishAmerica
Baltimore

Hardcover 978-1-4512-2719-2
Softcover 978-1-4512-2720-8
PUBLISHED BY PUBLISHAMERICA, LLLP
www.publishamerica.com
Baltimore

Printed in the United States of America

# OCTOBER

October, in the area surrounding Baronsville, Ohio, is a feast for the senses.

The night patiently waits for day to come. The moon light shrouds everything in its view. It wraps itself in a silvery silence. Even the stream of water, tumbling over the rocks in its path, quietly finds its flow. Birds clinging to the branches of a tree, and the sheep on the hillside, sleep the night in endless, soundless time.

Each day begins with a profound silence. The leaves on the trees and the grass in the meadows await the stirring of a gentle breeze to announce their gentle rustle.

Then, at the hint of dawn, a lone bird sings his call, then a moment of silence as if anticipating a reply. The song is repeated. Faintly, from a distance, comes the answer from another bird, soft, gentle like a tiny bell, clear and pure.

It's as if a magnificent orchestral composition is about to be heard. There is an expectant hush in the audience, as one lone tone of a bell begins the music.

Was not the same silence available in the rush of summer?

The sheep, in neighbor Jones' pasture, bleat their call to start the day. Their individual utterances seems to say, "Good morning. Did you sleep well last evening? The chill of this October morning announces the coming of winter." Clearly, each voice is recognized as if sounded by one's side.

Why does October serve such sensuous sounds?

As the sun peeps just above the horizon, the rolling hills become a painter's palette. The reds, yellow, and orange of the sugar and maple trees intensify with each second of the sunrise. A lone pine among the trees add vivid contrast in its green. Even the great oaks must await their turn when their rich, chocolate brown will cause one to consume the scene like a double chocolate sundae. What scene will Nature paint with such rich options of color?

The aromas of autumn fill the nostrils. How can the once beautiful leaves, now beginning their return to the forest floor, hold one's attention in their new state of being? Like bacon frying or an apple pie baking in the oven, this cycle of life stirs one's senses.

October days are chilled. The sun is warm. The contrast is as energizing as breathing in and breathing out. Or creating a painting with dark colors against light, a dancer's use of space, and the space awaiting to be filled, or the use of silence to release the tensions and the excitement of sound

October in all its sensuousness is a feast for one's being.

# CHAPTER 1

## *The Mitch Roberts Family Move*

The beginning of October was a time of struggle and demands on the Mitch Roberts family. Not desiring to continue to face the problems of the inner city, they purchased the Sam Dawson farm following Sam's death the previous summer.

The farm, located on the southwest side of Baronsville had been Sam's home for most of his eighty-eight years. Sam was most involved in the business of the community. He served many years on the Baronsville school board, then as a county commissioner representing his township. Sam was always present when someone in the community suffered severe problems. Sam's funeral was one of the largest every held at the Congregational Church.

The Roberts were to move into their new home on Saturday. Friday was spent overseeing the movers as they packed the furniture, dishes, glassware and mementos. Their son Jack was to be there on moving day to supervise the move.

Mitch began his day with a golf game, which he said was an important meeting with a client of the Supreme Food Company, of which he was a senior vice-president. He also informed his wife that he probably wouldn't be home for dinner, he'd probably have dinner at the Athletic Club. He often met with important clients there. That would be important if he were ever to become president of the company. He said they should check in at the Wayside Inn in Bloomfield and he would join them there, as all their furniture would be on the van, ready to be delivered at their new home on Saturday.

Mrs. Roberts and Jack oversaw the details of the preparation for moving. It was rather late in the day when the work was completed. The drivers of the moving van said they would be at the house in Baronsville around nine the next morning.

Jack and his mother checked in at the Wayside Inn and had dinner. It had been an exhausting day. They each went to their rooms and fell asleep. No one knew when Mitch finally made it to his room. This was not unusual. It had happened often.

Gladys didn't stir when he came into the room.

The family met for breakfast early the next morning. The conversation was sparse concerning what had happened during the golf game and dinner at the Athletic Club. Mitch was concerned about his getting to the golf course in time for his round of golf with a client from Indiana who came to meet with him. Would they mind if they went to Baronsville to oversee the moving into the house? They shouldn't wait up for him. He would probably have dinner someplace in the city. And with that he excused himself, grabbed his hat and jacket and left the hotel.

At eight in the morning. Mrs. Roberts and Jack, having had breakfast, went to their rooms, picked up their suitcases, checked out at the desk, got their car and began the short drive down the highway to their new home in Baronsville.0

They arrive in time to open the house to fresh air, its having been closed for many months. Pieces of furniture from Sam Dawson's days still inhabited the spaces. Someone had covered many of the pieces with sheets to protect them from the dust. Some will be stored in the garage behind the house; some will be given later to families who might find them useful. A yard sale may be needed in a week or two. A yard sale must be done soon to avoid the onset of winter.

As they considered all that must be done, they heard the sound of the moving van truck. Jack and Gladys went out to meet the men.

"We have a major problem, before we can bring in much of the furniture. The previous owner's things are still in the house. I'd really appreciate it if you could move all of it to the garage for temporary storage." began Gladys. "My husband had a golf game this morning, so I'm having to make decisions for which I hadn't planned."

"That's no problem, lady. Time is money for us. This is our only job this Saturday."

Jack took the keys and unlocked the garage doors. The transformations had begun. The men sized up each of the objects, retrieved their dollies, moved Sam's furniture out, and soon the house was empty. The sweeping of the rooms followed, and the Robert's household furniture and boxes were in their places in the house.

It was late in the afternoon when the movers left. Once the Dawson furniture was moved there were boxes to be opened and the contents placed in their rightful drawers or closets within the house.

Gladys dropped into the large chair in the living room. "Many of these things will have to wait until later. I'm just too tired to do much more. Sit down., Jack. You've really been helpful. I think we'll fix a bite to eat and get to bed early. I'd like to go to church in the morning and begin to meet the people."

Gladys had grown up in a village much like Baronsville and knew the importance of knowing and being known. In her village, as in most small villages, everyone knew everything about everyone. Right is right and wrong is wrong, and to become a part of the community, acceptance was determined by how you were known by those village rules and standards.

She also knew that her son, an athletic star in his former high school, would have to establish himself anew in their new community. There would certainly be young people in the First Congregational Church. What better place to meet the kind of young people she would like her son to know.

"What would you like to eat? It can't be too fancy for we haven't had time to shop for much food. How about a sandwich and some potato chips?"

"Sounds great, mom. I, too, am tired from all the lifting and moving of things. I'll probably do well to hit the horizontal early"

Gladys put together some slices of ham and cheese between slices of bread, while Jack tore open the bag of potato chips. It was nearly seven-thirty when the last morsel was consumed. They returned to the living room. Gladys picked up the Bloomfield Daily News and began to read. Jack picked up the racy novel a high school buddy had given him. While they were both initially interested in what they had chosen to read, they soon grew weary of the content.

Mitch Roberts had not yet returned from his sessions in the city. Jack noticed that his mother had fallen sound asleep with the newspaper in her lap. Jack tucked his book close to his body and quietly went up the stairs to his room.

Jack's room faced the southeast direction. They had taken the time to make their beds in anticipation of weariness. Eager to stretch his six foot six inch frame upon the bed, Jack began to shed his clothes. Pants were thrown across the back of a chair Meanwhile he was looking for his pajamas, but in which box were they packed?

Too tired to search, he decided that his sleep wear tonight would be his boxer shorts. Having gotten down to them, he turned out the light and went to the unclothed window to gaze upon what was beyond the house. There simply hadn't been time to see the ravenous colors of the trees, or to experience the sensuousness of October. The light from the full moon cast a silvery silence about him. Grotesque shapes appeared as shadows in the moonlight. Jack seemed to sense that all about him was in suspension. He had never felt this before. What was happening to him in this new setting?

Jack crawled into bed, pulling the cover up about him to disperse the chill of the night. Almost instantly he was asleep. Soon there was a warm berth about him. Once during the night he opened his eyes to review the stillness of the moon light before turning on his back to continue his sleep.

Sometime late in the night, or the beginning of dawn, he became lost in a dream. A beautiful young girl with long, golden blond hair entered his space. Her hair had an inner glow about it, as if it were filled within by sunlight. She was clothed with a sheer fabric that allowed one to see every curve in her body. Her breasts, young and firm, caught the fabric and caused it to stretch upward and outward. Oh, if I could only see her face, he thought in the dreams, but it was not to be. Then she lifted the sheet that covered his body and taking the tip of her finger began to touch the top of his forehead where his strong curly, black hair began, and traced down over his forehead, his nose and then three times across his lips. On down she continued to his chest where she delicately touched the tips of his nipples before proceeding down to his navel. Three times around the navel and then on downward.

As quickly as she appeared she was gone. In his half sleep he felt a surge beginning at the tips of his toes and then racing upward into what seemed an eternity before exploding through his whole body. For a very brief time he reveled in the warmth of the experience.

Then Jack became fully awake. "Oh, nuts, not again! What a mess!" Throwing back the covers, he stood up, deciding what needed to happen next.

First, take the shorts and wipe the mess from his body. Then there would need to be a shower. What was it that Grandpa Roberts once jokingly told him as a part of his sex education . "First you wash down as far as possible, then up as far as possible and finally—possible" Jack made his way to the shower in the bathroom down the hall. Glancing in the mirror and with a sense of the erotic, he thought to himself, "Much is possible in life!"

Sam Dawson, in his old age, did not find getting in and out of a bathtub an easy task. He had installed a shower in the upstairs bathroom for his convenience.

As he approached the shower, Jack glanced in the mirror at his body, pleased that the good Lord had amply endowed him with what they called his manhood. Jack quickly showered and dried himself before shaving.

The aroma of bacon cooking in the kitchen found its way to the second floor. Jack was ravenous. Breakfast couldn't come too soon.

"Jack, breakfast is almost ready. Hurry, son, your dad wants to get to the country club for an early tee time," his mother called. "How many eggs? How do you want them cooked?"

Not knowing where his clean shorts could be found, he slipped into his trousers, donned a shirt and socks and hurried to breakfast. There would be time to find the other items of clothing. needed to complete his dressing.

"Morning, dad. How did your game go?"

Ignoring the question, Mitch said, "Thanks, Jack, for helping your mother with the moving." Obviously the game had not gone well.

"I do wish you would spend some time with us, Mitch" Gladys continued. "I want to go to church this morning and get acquainted with some of our new neighbors. If we're going to live here we need to be a part of the community."

"Sorry, dear, I need to look after business for the Supreme Food Products Company. The board will never make me president if I'm not fully involved. I hear the president is about to retire and I might be next in line. We do enjoy the benefits from my salary," Mitch countered He finished his breakfast, and made his way to the door. Stopping, he said, "Don't know just when I'll get back this evening. It all depends on how well the business goes." And with that he was gone. No one really knew what all the "business" was,

Jack cleared the table, drew the water for washing the dishes and began the cleaning. His mother grabbed a dish towel, dried the dishes and stacked them ready to be placed on the kitchen shelves when she could decide where everything should go.

"I do hope we can meet some of our new neighbors at church. I'll get dressed. We should leave about ten-thirty. Church begins at eleven. I don't want us to make a conspicuously late entrance. I'd appreciate it, Jack, if you'd get the car when we're ready and drive us to church."

"Always ready to help, Mom, especially if I get to drive!" They went to their room to dress for the departure.

# CHAPTER 2

## *At the O'Connor Corner*

Craig O'Connor and his family lived in the house build by his great-great-grandfather shortly after the Civil War. Someone in the O'Connor family had lived there continuously since then. The family had been a major part of the building of the community. Craig's grandfather had helped to build the Congregational Church just across the street. Everyone in the family had been faithful members of the church and important to the shaping the values of the community. Craig's wife, Martha, was known by all as "Marty". Their only daughter, Carrie, had been born into the church community. What they had deemed as "right" most other people in Baronsville would agree was "right" and what was "wrong" was wrong.

On that first Saturday in October the Craig O'Connor family had spent a part of their day preparing the church for services on Sunday. There was always the sweeping of the carpet and the dusting of the communion table, the piano, and the pulpit. Everything must be in its proper place when the new day for church began. They would probably need to start the furnace to generate a feeling of warmth for those attending.

Each member of their family had their traditional task that was religiously done, week after week. So went each Saturday afternoon. When the church was cleaned, and locked up for the night, they would cross the street to briefly rest before Marty and Carrie prepared supper before early retirement and rest. Carrie and her mother had made a pot of navy bean soup. That, a salad, and some of Marty's homemade bread would be their supper.

All three of the O'Connors enjoyed their time together. There were always activities in which each member was included. Most recently, Craig had taken Carrie on a driving lesson, she having just gotten her driving permit. Earlier in the week they had gone to Bloomfield to see a family movie. Carrie, being their only child, was much protected, having been guarded against events that might harm her.

Following an evening of reading, they retired to their bedrooms. Carrie spent a time brushing her golden blond hair. Many of her friends admired the beauty of her hair. The habitual brushing of it helped to fix the radiance, as if from deep within. She carefully hung or folded her clothes before donning her new nightgown.

Carrie looked out her bedroom window to view the beauty of things clothed by the moonlight. As she looked out, everything seemed to come alive, to take on new life within a new nighttime setting. As she moved to her bed she thought to herself, "How could I be so lucky, to have parents who love me, and I them; that I have wonderful school friends who are always present when I need them. And this day, so rich with beauty and serenity, that can be a part of me."

Carrie stretched herself out on the bed, pulling the covers up to make a cocoon to ward off the chill of the night. Almost instantly she drifted off, surrendering herself to the promise of a new day.

The night passed too quickly as she began to respond to the sunlight edging its way into her room. She moved her foot away from the warmth of her acquired space, only to feel the chill and quickly draw her foot back to the warmth. As she lay there, she became aware of her own body. She could feel every wrinkle in the sheets. Even the buttons that held the mattress together entered her awareness. They seemed like giant objects to carry her to a place unknown or never visited before. As she reached down to draw the covers up more closely around her neck, she brushed her breasts. The sensation of touching her breast caused a sense of feeling she had not noted before. While there was such intense new feeling, it was only to be interrupted.:

"Carrie, time to rise!", father called from the bottom of the stairs. "Your mother has breakfast almost ready. Can you smell the bacon? "

"Coming, Dad. Give me a minute to brush my hair and comb my teeth. I mean, brush my teeth and comb my hair." With all these new sensations racing through her mind, she had trouble making sense out of what she was saying.

She quickly brushed her teeth and give a few swipes at her hair. There would be time later to do all this more carefully before dressing for church. Putting on her bathrobe and her slippers she descended the stair and into an embrace with her father. "Morning, mother. Breakfast smells heavenly. What's for breakfast?"

"French toast and bacon. Two or three slices?"

"Goodness gracious, only two! Young girls must watch their figures, if they expect the guys to watch!" She was amazed that such an expression came from her. Not at all the way she usually responded. She thought to herself, "What's happening to me!"

Craig O'Conner smiled, "Mom, I think our little girl is growing up. What do you think?"

She chose not to reply. "How many pieces for you, Dad?" Then teasingly, "You don't have to watch your figure. You're already caught!"

"Make it three and how about three pieces of bacon?"

"Coffee? Orange juice, Carrie?"

"Affirmative" came the reply from husband and daughter.

As they were served, they sat together holding hands, Craig began, "Let's pray God's blessing on this food, our family and all the people with whom we meet. Gracious God, we give thanks for this day, a good night of rest and the promise of this new day. Help us to be fully present to the opportunities afforded us. Now bless this food and she who prepared it. In your holy name. Amen."

Such a breakfast had been a ritual for more than the seventeen years they had been a family of three. When breakfast was completed, and the sharing of news of what was happening in Baronsville, they cleared the table. Dad washed the dishes while Carrie dried them. Their joy of being and working together was a wonder to behold. Marty returned the ingredients that were a part of the meal to their places on the kitchen shelves. When it was all completed they returned to their rooms to dress for church.

The awakenings of the morning were still filling Carrie's consciousness. She took a little extra time to choose a dress, one that would give contrast to her silky, blond hair. She brushed her hair a little extra to assure an aliveness as it covered her shoulders and down her back. She felt blessed that she was not troubled by blemishes on her skin; that it was smooth.

The three O'Conners, dressed for the morning, left their house about nine forty-five, in time for the morning Sunday School class. It would be here that Carrie would meet her girl friends and they could share gossip of the week. Carrie knew gossip wasn't right but it was such fun. How could something so much fun be wrong?

The family crossed the street to became a part of their larger family.

# CHAPTER 3

## *The Church Meeting*

It took very little time to cross the highway to the church. This early on Sunday morning, it was only a few cars and trucks that established a flow, and interrupted the silence. Even trucking is less heavy on Sunday morning. They entered the church, making sure that everything was still in its rightful place before each went on to his or her Sunday School class.

Carrie was the first to get to the class for high school students. In no time, her friends arrived.

"Have you heard the news?" Betty Baird asked excitedly. "I heard we're getting a new. student at the high school and he's a basketball star from Central High in Bloomfield."

"I even read about him in the Bloomfield News. They even had a picture of him in the paper." one of the girls added.

"What a hunk! I heard he's over six-feet tall. Boy, will that ever add to the Baronsville basketball team! He's obviously taller than the other guys on our team," another chimed in.

Geoffrey, a member of the team, listened without a word. "Do I always have to come in second best? Will I ever understand girls," he thought to himself. "After all, it's just fun to be able to play. Does the whole community have to come unglued over a ball game?"

The girls kept pretty much to themselves. A couple more guys arrived. Their the teacher, Gordon Brown, the local barber, arrived to teach the class. Seeing that something had created a lot of excitement, he decided to talk it out before they could get to the lesson for the day. "Alright, girls, what's all the excitement about?"

"You mean, you haven't heard? The Roberts family from Bloomfield has moved to Baronsville. Their son was a star athlete at Central High in the city. There was even a big article about him in the Bloomfield newspaper," Betty replied with excitement. "He's over six-feet tall! Imagine how that will add to our team!"

Gordon, looking at Geoffrey and the other guys in the class said, "Would it not be helpful to wait until we meet the Roberts and invite them into the activities of the church? We need to keep a perspective on what is good for everyone in our community." Mr. Brown paused, that each person could reflect on his suggestions. "Reverend Ryan's sermon topic this morning is on the scripture concerning love, First Corinthians, chapter 13." The admonishment caused a quieting of the group.

"Carrie, did Reverend Ryan call you to ask you to read the scripture in the service?" Mr. Brown asked. Carrie shook her head "no". "Perhaps we might practice reading it and have some discussing about the topic. Please open your Bibles to First Corinthians, chapter 13. Carrie, would you read?"

Carrie began to read with authority and feeling: "If I speak in the tongues of men and of angels, but have not love, I am a noisy gong or a clanging cymbal. And if I have prophetic powers and understand all mysteries and all knowledge, and if I have all faith, so as to remove mountains, but have not love, I am nothing. If I give away all I have, and if I deliver my body to be burned, but have not love, I am nothing. Love is patient and kind; love is not jealous or boastful; it is not arrogant or rude. Love does not insist on its own way; it is not irritable or resentful; it does not rejoice at wrong, but rejoices in the right. Love bears all things, believes all things, hopes all things, endures all things.

Love never ends; as for prophecies, they will pass away; as for tongues, they will cease; as for knowledge, it will pass away. For our knowledge is imperfect and our prophecy is imperfect; but when the perfect comes, the imperfect will pass away. When I was a child, I spoke like a child, I thought like a child; when I became a man, I gave up childish ways. For now we see in a mirror dimly, but then face to face. Now I know in part; then I shall understand fully, even as I have been fully understood. So faith, hope, love abide, these three; but the greatest of these is love."

There was a time of silence as each member seemed in deep thought. Geoffrey was the first to speak. "Wow! That's serious stuff! Does it mean I have to love everyone, even those who did dirty stuff to me?"

"What do you think it says? Do you think we get to choose who we love? What do you think love means in this instance?" Mr. Brown questioned. "As you become older, these words will call your values into question. It won't be easy. Life presents many challenges. Living out these suggestions for life cause me often to think and act responsibly. That's not always what I would like or what would be easy to do. In my adult life these thoughts cause me to do more reflection than almost any other ideas. Other questions anyone?"

Betty confesses, "One of the girls in my class shared some untrue gossip about me. I was furious but didn't know how to confront her. I kept the hurt to myself, but I found I didn't want to trust her. Our relationship has gone nowhere. We almost never say a word to each other. I know she knows why I avoid her. Do I have to love her?"

"I know how painful that is. I remember some events like that when I was in high school. When it was I who held the grudge, it was I who paid the price. I found myself not trusting others for fear of being hurt again. How simple it might have been to be able to say with caring, "Wow, that hurt. I don't know what to do with that. And I'm sure I don't want to spend my energies holding on to the hurt. I do value you as a friend and I want to be a friend in the future."

"Do I hear that having trust in others is important? How is it possible to build trust in a relationship?" Millie Matthew asked.

"I find when I trust people I really care about them. I find we have ways of sharing that caring," Geoffrey volunteered. "I also find myself complimenting them for the good things they do. That seems so easy."

"Affirmation and caring is essential to the building of trust. When we trust fully it's easy to create a relationship. If trust is not fully present problems may arise. Begin with affirmation and caring or in other words, love", Mr. Brown replied.

"That was such a great job of reading, Carrie. I liked the emphasis you put on the various ideas, and the space between each idea, to give them emphasis. There was time to think about the meaning of the words. If you read like that during the church service, the congregation will receive meaning of the scriptures."

"Goodness gracious, what's happened to the time? It's time we head up to church. Carrie, remember Reverend Ryan will be expecting you to read the scripture. Before we go, might we bow our heads in a moment of prayer? In the silence of your thoughts, take a moment to think about those moments when you felt most loved, and what happened in your relationship with others that you have cared about and were free to express your caring with them." In silence each person bowed his or her head and quietly waited. "Thank you, God, for these young people and the promises for their lives. Thanks you, also, for the beauty of this day and our opportunity to come together in your name. Amen."

The youthful energies were once more present when, with chattering and physical actions, the girls raced to the sanctuary. The boys walked slowly to their seats. Carrie chose a seat at the outside end of the row, so that she would be free to go to the front to read the scriptures. The girls sat together, with the boys a row or two behind them.

It was exactly ten-fifty when Jack and his mother arrived at the church. Jack carefully parked the car and joined his mother to enter the church.

As they came into the narthex, they were greeted by Mr. Brown and Mrs. O'Conner. "Welcome to First Congregational Church. I'm Gordon Brown and this is Mrs. O'Connor. We all know her as Marty.".

"Thank you. I'm Gladys Roberts and this is our son, Jack." she said as they extended their hands in greeting. "This church reminds me so much of the church of my youth."

"Here is a bulletin. Marty will take you to your seats and introduce you to some of the members of the church." With that they were ushered to a pew on the side away from the youth.

"That's him! That's him! That's Jack Roberts, the guy we read about in the paper." Betty almost shouted with excitement.

"Wow! What a hunk! Look at those shoulders," one of the girls observed.

"Oh, why didn't I get curly hair? Why do some guys get it all?

The girls could hardly sit still, so excited were they.!

Carrie didn't look up. She was reading the morning bulletin to know when she would be called upon to read the scriptures. "This is different," she thought. "The scripture being read after the sermon? Nothing looks familiar. Everything is changed."

As Jack and his mother sat down to prepare for worship, Jack glanced to the other side of the room. The sun shining through the gold-colored glass of the windows cast a golden glow on Carrie's long, blond hair. It seemed like the glow was coming from inside the hair. Jack caught his breath. "It's her. It's the girl in my dreams," he thought. Remembering what had happened at the beginning of the day, he felt a stirring in his body. "Oh, no. Not now!" he thought to himself as he felt the stirring in his groin. "But who is she? How can she look so much like the girl I dream of so often."

Mrs. Grace Ryan, the minister's wife, and the choral music teacher at the high school, began the piano prelude. .She created variations on the hymn "Amazing Grace" Church members half-hummed the tune as they quietly continued their conversations. When she ended the prelude, Reverend Ryan walked from his chair to address the congregation.

"Good morning, everyone. May God's blessings be upon you. I trust you have enjoyed God's handiwork, the beautiful, colorful trees in the village and about the countryside; the refreshing coolness of the air, and the sense that all is right in God's world.

Please open your hymn books to page 256 and join in the singing of 'Amazing Grace'"

Mrs. Ryan began an introduction to the song. The congregation began singing.

"Amazing grace, how sweet the sound, that saved a wretch like me" the song began. It being such a familiar song, many never read the words. When the song was finished, Reverend Ryan continued with the service.

Please join me in the responsive reading. "Oh God, creator of all things, we give thanks for the beauty of this day"

"Praise be to you, oh Lord." the congregation replied.

"For the sharing of love this day with those who come in your name."

"Praise be to you, oh Lord"

The responsive reading continued with the congregation repeating their phrase. They ended the reading with "Be present this day and fill us with your love."

Reverend Ryan moved quietly to the pulpit. He bowed his head in silence. It seemed almost too long. Some moved about slightly as if to respond to the discomfort of the silence.

Then from the back of the sanctuary came the shattering sounds of a gong and the loud crashing of cymbals. Reverend Ryan stood motionless; no change in his facial expression.

Silence continued. Members of the congregation shifted in discomfort. Again the silence was interrupted by the shattering sound of the gong and the crashing of the cymbals. No response from the pastor. Everyone looked around to see what was happening.

Down the aisle walked a black man and an Asian lady. They proceeded slowly and with dignity. They took their places in chairs at each side of the stage area. Not a word was spoken. Reverend Ryan raised his head and carefully looked at the members of the congregation,. but said not a word. Silence continued. People became less comfortable and looked around to see what would happen next.

Again there was the shattering sound of the gong and a crash of the cymbals.

Reverend Ryan now looked up and with a strong assertion began, "If I speak in the tongues of men and of angels, but have not love, I am a noisy gong or a clanging cymbal." Again the shattering sound of the gong and the crashing sound of the cymbals. "And if I have prophetic powers, and understand all mysteries and all knowledge, and if I have all faith so as to remove mountains, but have not love, I am nothing." The gong and the cymbals were heard more softly.

"You probably wonder why I have invited Lily Wong and Samuel Brown to share this service with me. You probably know Samuel as Sammy, the custodian at the high school. I want to share with you what I have learned about Samuel Brown. Before I was called to the ministry, my passion was theater. I loved the applause received following a great performance. I felt special when I could fully become the character I was playing. It was like my soul was awakened. Knowing that one must be exceptionally good to make it professionally as an actor, I decided that I should prepare for something I could do if I didn't succeed as an actor. I took classes to be a teacher. Today, if the Baronsville High School is in need of a drama or English substitute, I am pleased to serve.

What I discovered was that Samuel Brown is key in creating an open, caring environment at the high school. Mr. Brown knows the first name of every student in the school. As he does his work, he greets individual students warmly, with a smile and by their name. Because he is responsible for the whole school, he is often at the place where some difficulty occurs. He graciously, and with caring, helps to solve a problem. I have watched the number of times students would search for him to talk things out. Samuel Brown serves in love.

You probably know Lily Wong as the cook at Alice's Diner. How often have you chosen to eat at the Diner because Lily always created gastronomic delights. When we moved to Baronsville, we were quickly told about the great food at Alice's Diner. What you don't know is that Lily lives in the inner city in Bloomfield, a place of emerging problems. She drives here every day to serve us. But what you,also, may not know is that on her days off she conducts a Cooking School in her neighborhood, inviting youth to learn to cook, and, in the process, appreciate wholesome food. These young people probably don't realize that she teaches them to read as they try to bring to life the recipes she shares. Nor do they know she is teaching math as they carefully measure the ingredients for the dishes. She is building community as these young people work together to produce great menus, and how they learn to celebrate each other as they consume their creations. Lily Wong is love in action. So excellent is her reputation that young people who live far from the area where she lives have begun to ask to share in the school.

Both Lily and Samuel live a distance from our village but they come to serve in love.

Listen again to the words shared by St. Paul as we hear again the invitation found in Fist Corinthians Chapter 13. Carrie"

Carrie rose quietly from her place in the pew. She walked quietly, and with assurance, to the pulpit. She brushed away a tear before she began. Slowly and with intense feeling she began, pausing after each thought to allow the people time to reflect on the meaning of the words. The two high school band percussion players, softly played the gong and the cymbals each time those words, 'gong and cymbals,' were spoken. With the words "So faith, hope, love abide, these three; but the greatest of these is love," Carrie stood quietly and in reflection for a short time before returning to her seat. Once more the quiet, inviting sound of the gong and the cymbals was heard.

"Please join us in the singing of the first verse of 'Amazing Grace'." When the first verse was completed, Reverend Ryan once more addressed the congregation.

"You may have noticed that there is no offering to be taken in the service. Instead, you are invited to take whatever you would have given this day, and take it out into the community to serve someone in need. A gift without the giver is limited. A gift with the giver has power from on high.

"Mrs. Wong, Mr. Brown and I will be at the back of the sanctuary to greet you individually. Go in love." The three of them gathered together in an embrace and then quietly walked to the back of the sanctuary together. The high school percussion players once more struck the gong with a shattering sound, and with the loud crashing sound of the cymbals. The service had ended.

The usual post-service chatter was replaced with quietness. Little was said as they extended their hands in leaving. When the high school students left they each held Samuel's hand a little longer, saying without words, "Thank you!"

As Jack and his mother got up to leave, Jack asked, "Can we go to Alice's Diner for lunch? Maybe most of the members of the church will want to be there, too."

# CHAPTER 4

## *Monday Morning at the Diner*

Every morning many gathered at 6:00 at Alice's Diner for breakfast. It's a time to share news, although others might call it "gossip.". No one could remember who said what.

"Right chilly out this mornin'."

"Sweater sure feels good. Hope it warms up by noon."

"Did you see that someone's movin' into the Sam Dawson house?"

"I seen the movin' van there Saturday mornin' when I come into town for gas for my truck. I 'speck there was a lot of heavy movin' of things."

"Someone said Sam's stuff was still in the house when the new people bought it. Wonder what they'll do with all his stuff."

"Changin' subjects, how many of yous was at church yesterday? A mighty diff'rent service."

"First time I ever seen a church service that didn't take up a collection."

"The preacher wants each of us to take whatever we'd give to the church on Sunday and go out to help somebody in need"

Charlie Pitts, the church treasurer said, "Won't be much to help people from some of the members." Realizing he was about to share some private information, he quickly added, "That O'Connor gal sure did a great job readin' the scriptures. She's got a lota talent. Probably will go far in whatever she chooses."

"Did you see the new kid with his mother?"

"You mean that strappin' over six-footer? If'n he plays basketball, we may see more winnin' games this year."

"The people will love him if'n he changes the record of wins. Once when I was visitin' my sister in Bloomfield, we went to a Bloomfield Central High School game. He was somethin' else."

"Someone told me his old man was a vice-president of a food company in Bloomfield. "

"I think it was him I seen at the gas station this mornin'. Seemed in a hurry."

Gordon Brown came into the Diner to pick up his usual prepared lunch. "Morning, friends. Having a good day? Sure is beautiful out. October is one of my most favored times of the year."

"What time you openin' your barbershop, Gordon? My wife says that I better get a hair cut or she's gonna get me curlers!" Billy Burke said half jokingly.

"As soon as I can get the coffee pot going and get things straightened up. People are used to dropping by to chat and have a cup of home brew, coffee that is!"

Lily brought Gordon his usual ham and swiss sandwich, all carefully wrapped, and with some potato chips. Also tucked inside was a Lily cookie to top off his lunch.

"See you soon," as they waved him on his way.

"This community is really blessed with that man. My kids tell us so much about what happens in his Sunday School class"

"I'm a little uncomfortable with what the preacher asked us to do at the end of the service. How am I gonna find someone to go to? What'll they think if I go to someone I really don't know?"

"You're not alone. I'd bet everyone of us has some feelins' about that. What'll happen if we just don't do it? Who's gonna loose? Who's gonna know? I'll bet some of us just won't do it. There's always the excuse that we got too busy."

Alice served the Lily's special omelets and the attention turned to eating.

"Lily, this omelet is the most," Billy exclaimed. "If it tweren't so big to begin with, I'd probably order another."

"Right on, Billy," the chorus of guys loudly replied. "Lily, you're something else. How'd we get so lucky to have you keepin' us so well fed?"

"Oh, go on you guys. Butterin' is best kept to your toast!" Alice countered as she smiled with genuine appreciation for what Alice's Diner set out, and how so many had continued to be her customers.

"Gordon should have the coffee pot goin', I guess. Better get to his shop to get my locks shorn," Billy said as he left a tip, grabbed his coat and headed across the street to Gordon's Barber Shop.

# CHAPTER 5

## *Gordon Brown's Barbershop*

All businesses were on one side or the other, along Main Street. Gordon's shop was next to the Post Office, which made it convenient for people to drop by for a cup and some chatter after they had picked up their mail. There was only one customer to start the day, Billy Burch, the one whose wife said he had to get a hair cut or she'd get curlers.

Billy entered, threw his jacket over the back of a chair and quickly mounted the barber chair. "Just shorten it, Gordon. Gotta keep the wife happy." Gordon fastened the barber apron about Billy neck, and reached for the clippers.

The telephone rang. "Hello, Gordon's Barber Shop. Oh, hello Revered Ryan. You'd like a hair cut? Sure, things are kinda slow this morning. Just Billy Burch so far. Come on down. I should be available in about twenty minutes."

"That the preacher?" Billy asked. "He sure caught my attention yesterday in church. Can't remember a time when worship was so different; I jest find myself a little uncomfortable with what he's asked us to do. Ain't ever felt that way before."

"Why don't you stick around after we get done with you and maybe we'll find out more of what he's expecting?" Billy nodded his approval and Gordon continued the cutting of hair.

Reverend Ryan entered the shop, hung his coat on the hall tree, poured himself a cup of coffee, and sat down to await his turn.

"Morning, Reverend. Good to see you," Gordon began the conversation.

"The name is Richard, but most people call me Dick. And good morning to both of you. Good to see you, Billy. It was good to see you in church yesterday."

"A very diff'rent service. Caught my 'tention." Billy volunteered. "I tol' the guys at breakfast this mornin' that I feel uncomfortable with what you asked us to do. Not used to meeting people that'a way. What'll happen if I jest cain't do it?"

"Do what you feel is right. Everything happens in its own time. You weren't an adult the moment you were conceived, and you didn't have all those muscles when you were two" the Reverend said.

"And you didn't have this high forehead when you were in first grade," Gordon teasingly added.

"Let whatever you do be genuine. Let the action be something of which you can feel good about. It must come from the heart. It must be done in love," continued the reverend.

With that, Gordon removed the barber apron and held the mirror up for Billy to view his hair. "Right good job, Gordon. Guess the wife'll let me in the house. And think of how much I'll save not havin' to pay fer curlers!"

The Reverend took his place in the barber chair. Gordon fastened the barber apron about Dick's neck. Picking up the clippers, Gordon began. "I've been thinking a lot about the two guests at yesterday's service. It was an inspiration to hear of how they connected with the people in each of their communities. It's really impressive how meaningful a service can be without it costing much. Also, how important it is to give one's self to whomever one is with. I couldn't help thinking about Lily Wong and her Cooking School. The ingredients for the food must have cost something. How does she cover her costs?"

"That, too, is a wonder to behold. I also asked that same question. When I asked Lily she told me that Jim James, who owns the Supreme Food Products heard about her work and volunteered to supply the things she needed for free. It was Jim's grandmother and her cooking that started that company. When Jim's father was a child, his mother would make jams and jellies of the fruits collected in the wild. At first she just gave jars of the jams and jellies to friends and neighbors. They were so popular that people began to ask for her things. Jim's dad would take orders and deliver the things. The people, so grateful, would pay him for his work. He felt good about what he could share and the

38

monies he got. When his mother began adding pies and cakes to what they had requested, the possibility of a business began to happen. Jim James has not forgotten how the Supreme Food Products Company got its start, and the benefits that results when the motivation for what we do is right. Lily Wong's idea for service to the young people in her community appealed to Jim James. When he heard about what she was doing, he went to her and began his support of her work."

"Amazing story," Gordon said as the clippers continued to shape Dick's hair. "I must know more about Lily and her work. I close my shop on Saturday afternoon. Would you and Mrs. Ryan be my guests to go to Bloomfield, and have lunch with the students at Lily's Cooking School? Who knows, some of those students might enjoy a free haircut. I could take a stool and my barbering equipment, and, after lunch, the Cooking School could become a Barber Shop. How about it, Billy, like to go along and be my guest also?"

For a short time Billy was silent, then he replied, "Sure, I think it can give me some answers." Without another word, Billy lifted his coat from the back of the chair, then, pulling it about his shoulders, quietly left the shop .Going out, he turned to say, "Okay, Saturday, a little before noon. Thank you both."

# CHAPTER 6

## *Baronsville Basketball*

Jack, in part enamored by the memory of hearing Carrie reading at church and the memory of his dream and seeing Carrie flooded by the sunlight on the first Sunday at church, struggled to find a way to begin to know her better. "Don't I always get what I want?" he thought to himself. "Ain't I able to get what I want? Why am I so baffled by this? Other girls have been an easy capture. What's so different about this one?"

Jack's frustrations were worked out on the basketball court. He threw himself into the game with every ounce of his energy. The accuracy of his baskets increased. He was becoming a high scorer for the team, sometimes doing so to receive the applause of the people of Baronsville. Geoffrey and some of the other guys of the team were pleased to have won more games but were uneasy about the fact that it was often Jack's game and not that of the team.

Carrie would often attend a game, and enjoy the game when the team was truly working together. She applauded the whole team, and showed her appreciation for the work of each member of the team.

"Why can't she notice me? What do I need to do to get her attention?. She's so cute, so desirable! Why can't I get her out of my mind?" he would say to himself day after day. "Am I going nuts over this? Is this what the whole school year will be?"

And so the year wore on.

# WINTER

Winter announced its arrival early this year. The crisp crunch of the skiffs of snow is a reminder that life is taking on a new form. The bare branches of the sugars and the maple trees seem to lift their arms as if pleading for warmth and the blessings of spring. Even the few brown leaves on the oak trees hang lifeless to their branches as if not wanting to give up their once glorious existence.

Sheep on the hillside silently huddle together to face the winter's harshness. Their once clear bleating is replaced by the silent sound of snowflakes slowly settling down.

Some birds have chosen to escape to warmer climates. The songs of those braving the winter are in short supply. Their silence seems simply to await another time for celebration. Those who stay find comfort within the branches of the pine. Their hunt is for sustenance among the once rich colors of summer and autumn now turned to seed. Eagerly they partake in a process in which they assist in scattering the seeds to other settings that the glories of beauty be shared.

What is the purpose of winter? Is it to increase the desires for new life, having known a time of constraint, that Nature infuses a passion for spring? Is it that, intensifying the contrasts of seasons, spring will bear new, intense promise? Winter will come. All life must bear its burden. And in surrendering to it fully there is a fullness for the realities and readiness for spring. Everything must hold its place.

# CHAPTER 7

## *As Winter Bores On*

Mitch Roberts' schedule changed. His golf games were tabled. Some of his friends suggested they might supply him with red balls to be spotted more easily when the snow covers the golf course. Stopping in at the Athletic Club for a drink and some chatter with friends seemed less often. Some days the roads were icy and one had to drive more slowly and with greater care. Clients who once came to spend time with him were now less frequent. There was the need to fly into Cleveland or Columbus, rent a car and drive to Bloomfield. Mitch, uncomfortable with being at home, found it more difficult to find a reason for being away.

One week, during the high school vacation, Mitch decided that he needed to share with Jack the rules of the game in the business world. He wanted his son to be successful, at least as he had experienced success in his mind. He would let him experience the golf game, if the weather permitted, and he would certainly see to it that he would be introduced to what the Athletic Club is all about; that it is a place where one could exercise the game of power. Power, the ability to control, is how one makes it in the business world. How else could he ever expect to become president of Supreme Food Products? Maybe he could set Jack up to take his place when he retired.

That week never happened, although they often talked about business being a game; that it all gets played by unspoken rules. Even clients know how to play the game. Gladys would raise an eyebrow in disbelief when she heard such conversation. Mitch was always too busy, always striving to become more controlling. And, while he played the game, there were times when, deep within himself, he would search for a feeling of satisfaction. None of those inner feelings were ever shared. He must not appear weak or not in control. The game must go on.

Gladys continued her efforts to become more involved in the community. Mitch often told her she was wasting her time. She remembered the church service in which each person was invited to take their resources out into the community to help someone in need. Often she would take a meal to a member in the community who was unable to prepare meals for herself or himself. She felt good seeing the satisfaction that came from her simple efforts. At other times she would simply call a person who lived alone and share some friendly conversation. She began to prepare cookies and sandwiches for the time together with the members of the congregation following church.

Jack gave himself fully to be the star of the high school basketball team. He reasoned that people would like him if he displayed his real skill and control. Still, seeing Carrie O'Connor at school and at church, but receiving little encouragement for any deeper relationship, he became increasingly anxious of how to bring the two of them together. The thought of her filled many moments in his thinking. He thought of one thing after another in which they could be together and away from others. Still he felt reticent for just talking with her, in fear that she might reject him. He became obsessed by his desire for her. "The thought of her is driving me crazy", he often thought to himself. His prowess on the basketball court brought other girls to almost worship him. They could be easy conquests. "Why doesn't Carrie care for me?"

Winter continued on, requiring everything to respond to the limits imposed by nature. But with the limits there was only the intensification of feelings and desires. Winter was imposing its will.

Members of the village met almost every morning at Alice's Diner to share the happenings of the day. They often talked about the impact of Reverend Ryan's invitation to serve those in need in the community. Billy Burch shared that Carrie O'Connor had come by to baby-sit their kids while he and his wife went off to Bloomfield to see a movie, have a nice, quiet dinner at the Wayside Hotel, and just enjoy their time together. "We've had fun together. Musta been the haircut that I got right after that church service .in which we was asked to serve others. The 'little woman' has given up on the curler idea. I went with preacher and Gordon to see Lily Wong's Cookin' School. Made me do some thinkin' about what I could do with what I got."

Geoffrey spent more time talking with Gordon Brown. There was something in Mr. Brown's way of viewing things that appealed to him. One day he asked, "Mr. Brown, how is it that you have such great understanding of how we all get along together? You seem to see what makes things work and what seems to keep things from working. I'd very much like to develop that kind of understanding. Can you help me find what you seem to know?"

"I have a most enviable profession." Gordon began, "Each day someone from this community comes to get his or her hair cut. As I work, they share what's happening in their lives. Each day I am told what makes life seem to go right and what seems to keep it from being all it can be. I only have to listen and to invite them to become aware of what works for them and what keeps them from what they'd like in their lives. It's a kind of wisdom one gets from being involved with life. Some call it the wisdom from living."

Geoffrey continued, "I've watched carefully at the kinds of questions you ask in our Sunday School class and the kinds of observation you talk about as we ask serious questions. That's what I want to be able to do, to help people when they're in trouble."

"Know what, Geoffrey, the work load here is sometimes much. I've been thinking it would be good to add another chair and to have someone help with the work. Is that something you might like to do? I could help you learn the trade. Getting the wisdom is something you will have to discover for yourself. It comes easy if you will listen. What do you think?

Maybe what6 you might like to do is to be an apprentice in my barber shop. You could learn a trade while searching for your understanding of life."

"Wonderful, Mr. Brown. Sounds like a plan. May I stop in after school some days just to observe how everything comes together. I want to learn to listen and to hear."

Often during the week, when there wasn't a basketball practice, Geoffrey would stop in at Gordon's Barber Shop. Gordon would share with his customers what was happening, that Geoffrey would be apprenticing as a barber, and, as he worked, he would explain to Geoffrey exactly how he proceeded with cutting hair.

Then came the Saturday when Gordon explained, "Geoffrey, I'll be leaving for Lily Wong's Cooking School a little before noon on Saturday. I'd like you to go along. We'll take along a stool and the barbering equipment. After lunch we'll set up a Barbering School. You will begin your work. I'll be there to help you with the process. I'll wager you'll learn about life in the inner city as you work with the young people. Listening while working is key."

On Saturday, Geoffrey and Gordon Brown loaded the stool and the barbering equipment into Gordon's car and they set off for Bloomfield. Lunch was a delight. The students of the Cooking School served lunch with pride. They made sure their guests was treated royally and, following the serving, joined Gordon and Geoffrey at the table. They were filled with the excitement of having created a new dish that morning, an introduction to French cooking. The students were most pleased when their guests shared the utter delight in what they had tasted.

"How easy it is to connect with others when there is something that brings them together," Geoffrey thought to himself. . The food became an invitation to acceptance. How much the affirmation they had extended opened each member of the group to share his or her interests and details of their involvement with the school. Geoffrey listened.

When they had finished lunch, Gordon explained that as they had been learning to cook, Geoffrey was interested in becoming a barber. He shared with them that this was Geoffrey's first time of cutting hair and he, Mr. Brown, would be standing by to make sure that it would be safe for them to leave when Geoffrey had finished.

Trust had been established. One of the male students volunteered. Everyone of the students from the Cooking School watched intently and with appreciation for Geoffrey/s first time of cutting hair. When it was over and Geoffrey handed the mirror to the student, there was applause from everyone. The student smiled and extended a hand of appreciation for that for which he had been a part.

"Perhaps the Barber School can become an extension of Lily Wong's Cooking School," Geoffrey thought to himself. "I like the good feelings for what I've done. I must wait to share the idea with Mr. Brown. I know the real sense of good feelings comes when I give myself away."

Winter became more intense, more demanding of a person's resources. Winter bore on.

It was Christmas before Jack could get his courage up to reach out to Carrie. He felt awkward, not knowing what to say or do. "A gift. I'll give her a gift. Maybe she'll look my way. But what'll I give her?" Jack thought to himself. For days he struggled with what gift would most please her. When his family went into Bloomfield, he would secretly look at things that might please a young girl. Desperate and not able to find an answer, and seeing a display of perfumes, he smelled each one trying, to find the one that was most like Carrie. He settled on one that he thought would smell good on her. "I'll take that one." he said to the clerk. "It's for a girl I am becoming very fond of. Do you think it's a good one for a young girl?"

"Oh yes, sir. I know I'd love to receive it, especially from such a handsome young man!" With such flattery and reassurance, Jack almost burst with excitement as he paid for the perfume and had it gift wrapped. "I can almost smell it, when Carrie adds it to the smell of her own body," he thought to himself. "Oh, to be close enough to her and breath deeply into the mixtures of those smells." He lifted the perfumer bottle to take in the aroma, as he thought about what it would be like when Carrie was wearing it.

And there was the time when a group of students from the Sunday School class decided as a group to go to a movie. Jack made sure that Carrie ended up sitting next to him. Carrie was wearing the perfume he had given her at Christmas. The aroma was intoxicating. He was beside himself. He became aware of the erection emerging in his groin. At one point, he reached over, taking Carrie's hand, drew it to his lap and his erection. She quickly withdrew her hand aware that this was a new experience. "Is that what happens to boys?" she thought. "Not at all like what mother explained to me when she talked about sex and creation of life. This is very different. Why am I feeling something I've never felt before? I am suppose to know this is wrong but is it all wrong? What is life all about?"

Jack had started attending the high school Sunday School class. He often sat alone, unsure of how to express his feelings for Carrie to her. The guys in the class did not reject him but neither did they become open and friendly with him. His individual stardom on the basketball court, and the attention given him by some of the girls in the class, did not create a rich trust between him and the guys. Carrie had maintained a distance between them, remembering the night at the movie. Jack seemed unaware of the chasm that was developing between him and the other boys in the class.

Geoffrey spent more time listening. He began to hear what wasn't being said; what was not said. He was becoming aware of the attention Jack held for Carrie. That was not a good feeling. Geoffrey was most pleased by the sensitivity Carrie had for creative things, and her ability to express herself when invited. He knew the values of the family and the good for which they stood. He was moved by her beauty as well. Caring for Carrie was happening.

Carrie held to her desire to continue her education, to go to college and become one who might serve her community. There was the option of becoming a teacher, to work with very young children. Since knowing Reverend Ryan, the thought of writing or something in theater seemed to excite her imagination.

When Reverend Ryan would substitute for an English class, she would be affirmed for her writing of poetry. The Reverend would often say, "Carrie, that is beautiful. Your thoughts, expressed in verse, share the deep insights you have for human nature. I hope you continue your writing." Gradually her observations of events in the village became the topic of a poem. When she went for a walk in the meadow at her uncle's farm, a simple wild flower or the bluster of a winter snow became an interpretation of the beauty of life. Carrie would respond to the fullness of life and all its promises.

Geoffrey became fully aware of the sensitivity Carrie possessed and her ability to share it. It seemed so in tune with what he wanted, being an apprentice to Mr. Brown, in his quest of learning to know others more fully. He hoped that their each search for meaning would bring Carrie and him together. Where did such a thought come from?

Jack's passions became like a large snow drift in winter. While it mounted,. it remained cold and unmoving except when forced by the passions of a winter storm. Even applause of his athletic feats left much to be desired. All the affirmations for his physical prowess was not fulfilling. "How can I feel so much but get so little," he often thought to himself. "What will bring me satisfaction?" And while those questions came into his thoughts at times, they were quickly cast aside for his desire for Carrie. Those recurring night-time dreams simply added to his frustration. Carrie's face now was in the night-time dream.

Geoffrey, becoming more aware of the spoken and the unspoken messages, was increasingly aware of Jack's moods and actions. "Why doesn't he celebrate the gifts he gives to our team and the school? What more can one person want? What is it he wants from Carrie? I'm aware of some special feelings he has for her, but where does it lead? What is it he wants from Carrie? "

While he was increasingly aware of unspoken messages, Geoffrey could not understand the issues being observed. One afternoon after school he headed for the barbershop. Not a soul was in sight Geoffrey sighed a sense of relief. "Now I can ask Mr. Brown some of these  confusing questions," he thought to himself. He walked directly to Mr. Brown's barber chair, blopped himself in it, and gripped the arms of the chair as if to anchor himself. In the midst of his confusion he began, "I'm really puzzled by what is happening in our Sunday School class."

"What are you observing? Does it seem like there is a potential problem?"

"I'm not sure. Things just don't feel right," Geoffrey replied.

"Be more specific, Geoffrey. I don't think I understand."

"Something has changed since Jack Roberts has become a regular member of the class. I'm aware that when he comes he tends to sit alone, apart from the rest of the group. His silence is loud. Why can't he be more a part of the group? When we're in a game there seems to be little actions between the guys and Jack. In the class nothing seems to be happening. I just don't get it."

"May I ask you some pointed questions?" Geoffrey nodded his approval. "How have you invited him to be a real part of the guys in the group, with the other members of the group? Each of us need to hear an invitation to become involved. On the basketball court Jack experiences his own power. He can quietly respond to his sense of worth in his ability to make a basket, support others of you in playing the game. He knows where his own power comes from. Do we know much about Jack and his own experiences in groups like our class, in the subject matter being discussed? Do we know Jack? The power each of us were given may become a means to an invitation. It may be used to empower others, or, without intent, be used as a means to loss of helpful power and end up in control. It is a most important lesson to learn. It is the means to creating a group, a community."

"I must confess that there is a part of me that is jealous of Jack's athletic ability. When the girls of the group get so excited in being in his presence, the star of the basketball team, I find that difficult to take. The resounding applause for every basket he makes and our ability not to be as accurate hurts. There is a part of me that wishes he might never have come and that things could remain as they used to be. I know that's not right. It makes me so uncomfortable, knowing that those feelings are not right. I would guess that some, or maybe all of the other guys, have some of those same feelings. We've never talked it out, so it just lies somewhere in our minds."

"You are wise beyond your years. That is often a problem with many communities. People just don't want to deal with potential problems associated with change. We often hold on to things that no longer serve us. We have difficulty with things that are in conflict with what we value. Because we don't confront problems and deal with them they grow and become like a germ that infects the whole body. "

"I think I understand, at least in part, what you're saying. It's a difficult problem. I don't know where to start. What do I do with my feelings? How do I become honest with those feelings? I fear a part of me will not be open as long as I have those feelings."

"Begin by owning those feelings. Either you own them and are able to let them go, or the feelings own you and you'll always keep the struggle. What do you think would happen if you went to Jack and you said,'Jack I need to share with you what's going on in my head. I've been talking with Mr. Brown and he said that if

I were to find a way of getting to know you, I must begin with myself and the feelings I have. I have a great appreciation for your skills of the basketball team . There is a part of me that is jealous of your ability. I have not known what to do with those feelings. I would like it if we were closer friends. I would like it if we were more like a family here in church. Will you be my friend?' How do you think Jack might respond?"

"Wow! That will take lots of courage. What if he doesn't want to be a friend? What would I do then? Rejection is a bitter pill to take."

"Then the choice is one you must make. Do you want to keep those old feelings, or is it worth it to let go of those feeling in order to have a new relationship? We can never be responsible for someone else's actions. That is their responsibility. You will have done what is needed from you. When someone new comes into a community, the community begins to change." Gordon continued.

"Much to think about. I have to think this one through. I do know that how I express my feelings must be honest, the feelings must be my own. I hear your suggestions that I must begin with owning my feelings, letting them go, and create an invitation to a new relationship. Thank you, Mr. Brown. As usual you have been very helpful. I need to work this through, to practice what I have to say, to make sure the words are honest, and that Jack will be able to hear me."

With the conversation finished, Geoffrey rose from the chair and quietly left the barbershop, not saying a word, but caught up in the depth of his own thinking.

Geoffrey stopped in at Alice's Diner for a coke and some time to think. He was all alone. Not another of his circle of friends were there. He ordered the coke and began his internal dialog. "Why am I so uneasy with Jack? I have watched his attention to Carrie. What is going on there? What is his intent? Why is that such a concern to me? What are my feelings for Carrie? Am I in competition with Jack when it concerns my feelings for Carrie? Mr. Gordon tells me I must own my own feelings. Why can't feelings be resolved easily?"

Alice brought a coke to Geoffrey. "You look deep in thought, Geoffrey. Is there a problem? "

"Growing up and learning to think things through is sometimes a problem. Mr. Brown says 'I must own my own feelings'

"Many of us must work through those moments. I had to learn to trust the future. Lily tells me wonderful things about your work with the other students at her cooking school. Life often calls us to give ourselves to that which we believe in," Alice removed the extra place setting and continued.

"My having this Diner is much more than a place to serve Lily Wong's great food. It's a place where people can come together, share their lives, and work through problems that face us as a community. It's amazing what happens when conversations occur over a cup of coffee, a coke, and some choice of food. I can't solve the problems of someone else, but I can provide a place where the small problems of life can surface. Most often they never develop into large difficult problems. And when I really know another person and accept them, the differences matter less."

"Alice, you sound more and more like Mr. Brown" Geoffrey took a long sip from his coke and continued. "What a great treat it is to have people around who can help each of us begin to know ourselves and to help understand our lives. I didn't know why I wanted to stop in for a coke but perhaps a part of me was looking for the very thoughts you share." Geoffrey heard the last rattle of the straw at the bottom of his coke glass. "Thank you. Alice. You've been very helpful." Geoffrey pulled his jacket about himself, left money for the coke, a tip and began his trek home.

"Trust. How can I really trust? Who do I trust most? Why do I trust some people more than others? Are my personal feelings connected to my ability to trust?" As he walked home, the questions kept rushing through his mind. Are there questions that seem difficult to be posed? The time to walk home seemed shortened by the presence of the thoughts, and with the ideas shared with him.

Geoffrey quietly entered the house, going to his room, and getting out his homework. There seemed comfort in knowing what and how to do the task before him.

# SPRING

Winter is, at last, losing its grip on the control of life itself. Like a child peeking from behind her mother's skirt to see if it is safe to come out, the bulbs of crocus, daffodils, and tulips push out to see it it is time to show themselves in full dress, and with all their glory. Days when the last reminders of winter assert themselves with a light spring snow, the plants declare themselves and the intent to which they will become. Even the large barren leaves of the oak trees decide that the time has come, they can relinquish their vigil and descend to the place from which their life began.

With the promises of spring, even the softness of the spring air seems to invite one to fully disrobe and to be enveloped by the sensuality of the perfumed, gentle breezes. The earth is thawing. Blades of grass stand taller, showing off their greenness, their prediction that everything is about to be engaged, and declare their every desire. In that act, one is reminded that all of life comes together by the forces of Nature. Blades of grass become a feast for mother sheep as they give birth to lambs. Lambs bounce about in celebration of their being. The robins return. Earthworms, having spent their winter interned in the spaces below the frost line, emerge to provide lunch for the flocks. Like a great orchestra, all the instruments of nature execute their sounds to the Great Conductor. The symphony of life is beginning its first movement.

Can anything hold back what Nature has declared is life? But the weeds also find new life Will they hide the flowers, or crowd out the beauty of what might be? Is their purpose to show the contrast to the beauty inherent in what one knows is right? Who will bear responsibility for what is right? Is there to be responsibility in viewing and experiencing the good in life? Is it right that a thistle, fully grown, might overcast and hide a tulip? Is it possible that, in the quest to experience all that spring has to offer, the abandonment to desires may bring a full life into question?

Spring. What does it bring?

# CHAPTER 8

## *Finding New Life*

Spring suddenly erupts to declare winter is over, time to burst forth with the energies of what is at the center of life. There are still challengers, experiences that must be overcome. The spring rains, with the thawing of the snow, insist their conditions must be tolerated. After all, they are the means to the flowers, later adorned with color and fragrance.

Morel mushrooms, caught by the emergence of warm weather, shoot up in wooded areas, as if hiding from those who marvel at their taste, and who are committed to finding them. Asparagus, their roots resting for the winter, come forth to tease the pallet. Everything seems poised to feed the body and the soul.

Geoffrey waited to meet Carrie at the end of the school day. "Carrie, would you join me for a coke at Alice's Diner? I'd just like to share what's been going on in my head"

"I'd like that. I have been thinking a lot about what I want to do with my life. I'm not sure that everyone would understand my dreams."

"Great. May I carry some of your things? What's a man for, anyway!" he said with a chuckle. "Let me take those books." Together, they comfortably walked up the street to Alice's Diner. Neither said much but seemed to be deep in their own thoughts, as if each was unsure of just how to begin the conversation in this new, emerging relationship.

When they arrived at the Diner, Geoffrey stepped ahead to open the door. They entered and found a booth at the corner of the dining room, away from the other persons finishing their coffee.

Alice watched from near the cash register. She thought to herself, "I've seen this happening before. In fact I remember a time with a new beau when we didn't know how to begin a conversation. It was a most awkward moment."

Alice made her way to the booth with two cokes in her hands. "Getting here at 4:24 is the magic moment. The cokes are on the house for customers arriving at that very moment." she said, "And because this is at 4:24 on Thursday, there is a bonus of a tin roof sundae, guaranteed to put a dent in your supper appetite. I'll be right back. A bit of food helps to get a conversation going."

Geoffrey began, "She's amazing. Earlier, when I stopped in for a coke, she shared so much in a short time. She said that her Diner is more than a place to serve Lily Wong's great food. That it's a place where people in Baronsville come together to share their thoughts and to really get to know each other." He reached across the table and took Carrie's hand in his.

He continued, "I can't tell you how often I've thought about your reading of the scriptures when the service was about sounding gongs and clashing cymbals"

Geoffrey felt the gentle response in Carrie's hand. He knew they were relating. "I was very moved by the depth of your reading. It seemed like you savored every word, that it was to be felt as well as being heard. I had known you as a member of the Sunday School class and a classmate at the high school, but then I began to know you. I liked that feeling. On that day I knew I must know you better."

Carrie continued, "That was a very important day for me, also. I liked the feeling of being valued, of being invited to read. The whole experience was so intense. It was also important the conversations that followed. It seemed we were reaching for more than we had known before. I watched you and heard the questions you asked and the observations that Mr. Brown shared." Carrie's voice grew in its intensity.

"Then, I heard about your working with Mr. Brown and of your visits to work with the students at Lily Wong's Cooking School." Carrie beamed with approval. "I, too, have grown in my desire to know you better"

Alice returned and quietly set the Tin Roof Sundaes before the two and left without saying a word. The purpose of Alice's Diner was once more being met.

Carrie and Geoffrey didn't say another word, as though they didn't want to break the spell that was happening Between bites they would look at each other with a feeling of satisfaction for having gotten their relationship to a deeper level. And it felt right.

The last peanut, the chocolate syrup and ice cream were history. Geoffrey broke the silence. "We probably better head for home. Our parents might be wondering what happened to us. Now to pretend an appetite for the family supper.!."

Geoffrey left a tip at the booth. "Thank you, Alice. That was a very special treat."

Alice smiled. "You're welcome," She thought to herself. "It's amazing what a coke and a bit of food can do! What an investment for the future."

Carrie and Geoffrey smiled at each other. Geoffrey picked up Carrie's books, and opened the door to the restaurant. "I'm walking you home."

Their steps appeared to be lighter, as if they could take off skipping at any moment. When they arrived at Carrie's home there was one brief uncomfortable moment. Geoffrey was unsure what to say or how to separate. He didn't know how to express the feelings he was having for Carrie. In desperation he took her hand and said, "Thank you for one of the best moments I've had in my life. I hope there'll be many more coke sessions at Alice's." With that he handed the books to Carrie and went bounding down the street to go home.

Carrie stood quietly watching him until he was out of sight. With a smile as wide as the whole world she entered her home.

Carrie almost floated into the living room, tossing her books and homework on a table.

"Well now, what is this all about? Have you suddenly gotten wings and no longer need your feet to move you about?" her mother asked.

"Mama, I just had a coke and a tin roof sundae at Alice's Diner with Geoffrey," trying to hide her feelings."Alice just treated us to a coke and a sundae."

"I can't remember ever blushing after having a sundae and a coke!" her mother said with a knowing smile.

"Oh, okay. It was more than a coke and a sundae. Geoffrey told me how much he liked my reading of the scriptures the Sunday we introduced Lily Wong and Sammy Brown in the church service."

"Someone telling you that you did something well is a cause for blushing?" her mother asked .

"Well," Carrie now blushed in full color, "Geoffrey held my hand while he talked to me. And after we finished our treats, Geoffrey suggested we better head for home, lest our parents would be worried about us."

"And…." her mother said, inviting the conversation to continue.

"Well, we were both feeling something we hadn't felt before. We didn't know how to say 'good-bye' and how to part" Carrie blushed even more.

"And…" Marty O'Conner said, inviting the conversation to continue.

"I stood there on the porch, watching Geoffrey until he was out of sight. I'm not sure whether we was walking or just floating away. Oh, mama, he's such a special person."

Craig O'Conner was listening from behind the newspaper, which was, by then, a shield between himself and the two most important women in his life. At last he dropped the paper to say, "Well, mama, it seems our little girl is growing up. Do you remember when we began our falling in love? Their story warms this romantic elder's heart."

Carrie took comfort in what she heard from her father and mother.

Dad continued, "I, too, have noticed how grown up Geoffrey is. When I've gone to Mr. Brown barbershop, and Geoffrey has been there, I've heard the kind of questions he asks of Mr. Brown. They are most adult thoughts"

"Carrie, get your father to the table. Supper's ready."

"Come on, Daddy, get those bones moving." Carrie said, taking the newspaper from his hand, folding it, and giving it a light touch on the top of his head.

"Don't be beating your old man like that, young lady!" And with that he lept from his chair, throwing his arms about her, and saying, "Supper with your parents can't hold a candle to a coke and tin roof sundae, but let me tell you, young lady, I've done most wonderfully well on what has been put in front of me from your mother's hands!"

They seated themselves at the table, bowing their head. "Carrie, would you ask the blessing?"

"Sure, Dad."

"Thank you, God, for the blessing of this day, for all the promises spoken and not spoken, and for the joy that been given to us. Now, bless this food to our use and us in Thy service, for we ask it in your holy name Amen."

# CHAPTER 9

## *Meanwhile At the Robert's Home*

The basketball season has ended. Jack begin his quest for purpose in being. Will it be to give himself to baseball? And what about Carrie? The girl in his dreams continue to visit him; to remind him of his youthful maleness. He sees Carrie's face in his dreams. His desire for her increases.

Gladys plans a surprise birthday party for Jack's eighteenth. She invites the students from the high school Sunday School class, and some of the high school basketball team. And, of course, Gordon Brown, and the school basketball coach, to make the group complete.

Jack secretly hoped that the party could be smaller, and that Carrie would be an important person to be there. School would soon be history, and he'd have to find a job. But that might take him away from Baronsville, away from Carrie. "If only we could be together and alone. I must find a way."

Mitch is once more his contented self. The golf course is again in full swing. The greens are barely moved when he is there to tee off. He dreams of how he might become the president of Supreme Food Products. They are foremost in his thinking,."Gotta show the financial gain from my efforts, even if it costs some employees. Money is power, and I want power," he thought to himself as he swung his club to direct the ball. "Damn, it went in the rough. Gotta keep my mind on what I'm doing. Must keep my mind on what I want."

Gladys asked Jack to spade a patch of ground behind the garage so she could plant a garden. She loved the vegetables she would grow. She planted lettuce, beans, radishes, sweet corn, and set out tomato plants, cabbage and bell peppers. Carefully, she attended her garden every day. At the first sign of radishes peeping out of the ground, she became ecstatic. "Jack, come an' look, the seeds are beginning to grow. I can't wait 'til we have new lettuce for a spring salad. Seeing new life begin to emerge in its own time is a joy in heaven. Don't plant seeds until the possibility of frost is past."

# CHAPTER 10

## *At the O'Conners*

Carrie's family continued their service to the church and the community. Carrie would often take walks in a meadow to listen to a stream of water making its way to a fuller life. Taking her note pad and a pencil she wrote

Little stream in the meadow,
Let me hear your song.
So quietly you move
Yet your force is so powerful
When shaped in concert with other streams.

To be like your flow
Let me know,
That in my quietness
I can sense my power, deep within.

Flowing onward you feed
Each plant and shrub along the way.

Freely given, freely received
We know the beauty of your being.

Carrie shared her poem in the English class, when pastor
Ryan was substituting. Geoffrey was moved by the sensitivity of
her thoughts. "What beauty, as though coming from within her,."
Gwoffrey thought to himself. "A sensitivity much like that of
Gordon Brown. How can she possess such sensitivity and find
beauty in her writing? If only I could express myself so well."

Mr. Ryan invited Carrie to read her poem again. "Sometimes
we need to listen to hear what lies beyond the words, when we
grasp the feeling, at the center or the language. Read it once more,
Carrie. Give us time to become at one with the vision of your
words."

Jack heard little of the poem. His mind was filled with other
visions, the memories of Carrie, as the young blond girl who often
visited him in the night in his dreams. "I ache for her. She is always
in my thoughts. What can I do? How can this all end?"

Geoffrey stopped by the barbershop on his way home. He
needed to share with Mr. Brown what he heard in Carrie's poem,
and to share some some of his feeling coming from that time.
"Mr. Brown, I heard her poem, but I heard more than the words.
I don't know how to explain what I was feelin'. It was as though,
for a moment in time, I became at one with her words, and in
becoming at one with her words, I felt more of Carrie than I had
ever felt before. What is it all about? I can't explain it."

"Trust those feelings, Geoffrey. The depth of such feelings in
wha6t brings people together. When we care about each other

and celebrate each other', we begin to understand life and all its wondrous possibilities. Don't deny such feelings. Try to understand them and to know they are an invitation to something of great value. They are an invitation to life."

Geoffrey sat himself in the new barber chair, recently installed, knowing that Gordon Brown had just shared some of his wisdom for living. Gordon continued, "Don't rush into what will follow. Give it its own time, let it ripen into what it was meant to be. We don't harvest the grain in the field until its time has come. Forcing harvesting before the grain has ripened will not produce that which brings life for which it was meant to be. Often our inability to understand that simple truth will bring undesirable results. Live for honesty, truth, and love. Or was it faith, hope, and love. And the greatest of these is love?"

Geoffrey left his place on the chair and thoughtfully left the shop.

"That young man is in love. The feelings are so deep, so profound, he has yet to be fully aware of what it will demand," thought Gordon Brown, as he swept the floor to remove the clumps of hair, the results of service to previous customers. It being late in the day, and no other customers were in sight, he drained the coffee pot, emptied the grounds in the waste basket with the hair, shook out the barber's apron, folded it ready for the next day, turned out the lights, and locking the doors, began his walk to his home.

Jack hurried home. There was only one thing in mind. There was something about Carrie O'Conner that would not leave him. How often, recently. had his dream of the girl with the golden blond hair also had the face of Carrie. Those night-time dreams and the resulting physical responses only intensified his desire for her. The intoxication of the springtime perfumed air only increased his desire. Several days of the warm spring sunshine had created a blanket of soft green grass in the meadows. "Oh, to be there alone with Carrie."

And then the night time dreams changed. No longer was it just the girl with long, flowing, blond hair, the sheer gown and the face of Carrie. In the dream, the girl of his dream came in, removed her gown, and lifting the covers, crawled into bed with him. Her breast brushed across his chest. She put her fingers on his lips, as if to silence him from speaking. Sh cuddled closer with the curves of her body resting on him. As quickly as she came into his presence, she was gone. Once more he felt the surge rising through his body, and the eruption that was to follow. Jack lay motionless for a time, wanting to fully savor the experience of his dream.

"Oh, how I wish it might have been in real life," he thought to himself. "Why can't I get her out of my mind? Will I ever really experience the dream? How long can I control my feelings? Will she ever come to me? The distance from her only make my desire greater."

Carrie's imagination was filled with words and thoughts. Seeing the thrust of springtime energies often resulted in poetry about life itself. She would take her writings to Reverend Ryan to receive his praise for her creativity. "You have a great future with your writing. Your ability to share that quality with young children would be a most graceful gift. I trust that college, and if you prepare to be a teacher, it will become a reality. Continue your writing. No one can take that away from you. It comes from deep within your soul."

It was Saturday morning. Many of the villagers had stopped in the barber shop, following breakfast at Alice's Diner, for second cup of coffee and a bit of chatter. At last no one else came. Gordon poured himself a cup and settled into a chair to read the Bloomfield News. He had hardly gotten started reading when Geoffrey came rushing in. Geoffrey had become increasingly involved with his apprenticeship with Gordon Brown. It was often difficult to distinguish when the instruction was about barbering and when it dealt with understanding people.

Gordon began. "In a matter of weeks you will no longer be a student at the high school. But, like all of us, you will continue to be a student. You will continue to search the questions that become the base for how you grow. When we stop asking deeper, more significant questions, our growth slows down. Change is the result of questions. Always ask the 'why' of issues. That was something you probably did when you were a small child. Many parents sometimes feel frustration when their child keeps asking 'why', A small child's questions are essential to their understanding. Do you remembers the questions you asked of me, when we began our relationship more deeply? Did either of us know how those questions would bring us to this conversation?"

"But sometimes it's so difficult to find the question. Finding the right question was not what our classes in school were often about. I have to learn to learn differently. I'm often aware of what is happening. I just don't know 'why' it's happening," Geoffrey volunteered.

"Most people are unaware that being a barber,.and hearing the stories unfold while in the chair, requires asking the 'why' question. Now, looking at that mop on the top of your head, I think it's time to shore your fleece. I'll talk through the process one more time. Now do you know why I'm about to cut your hair?"

"Is the question,'Why do I need to know how to do the job?' I'll have to think about your 'why' question."

Geoffrey left his chair, settled himself in Gordon's chair, waiting for the barber apron to be tucked in and to hear the clippers begin their will practiced routine.

"Can we go back to Bloomfield to visit Lily's Cooking School? What is the payoff for Lily Wong? She does it for free, doesn't she? What does she gain?" Geoffrey asked. "That's a lota work just to do something for free."

"See how easy it is! You've started the journey. Yes, we'll go back. You need to study the young people she's working with. She lives in that community. What do you know about the youth who live there? What is their life like? Why did I take you on as an apprentice in my barber shop? Why does she want to teach them to cook? As soon as I finish your job, we'll grab the stool, the barbering equipment and head for Lily's. What new thing will we see today? Always look for the growing edge. That is what we'll build on!"

When they arrived at Lily's Cooking, all the students were deeply engaged in creating a quiche dish. They were preparing lunch for their benefactor, Jimmy James, the owner of Supreme Food Products, who had supplied many of he ingredients needed for the school. They observed a new face assisting Lily. He had rolled up his sleeves, donned his hat and apron, and was most involved in helping one group of students making pie crusts. Others were cooking bacon to be crumbled into the pie shells, while some were cracking eggs and beating the ingredients that formed the custard. Another group was shredding the cheese that would give the quiche more body and flavor.

It was a marvel to behold. Mr. James had informed Lily that he had invited the mayor and city council of Bloomfield to join him for lunch. When Jimmy had told his son, Gerald, a member of Supreme Foods staff charged with book-keeping and financial matters, Gerald had decided to lend his hand and join Lily in her supervision of the work.

Gordon and Geoffrey watched intently as the group became a force for good food. Those who had finished making and rolling out the crusts, began to set the table. Several of them had greeted Geoffrey warmly, having remembered their first meeting and his first adventure in cutting hair. Geoffrey quickly washed his hands, drying them, and gathering plates, glasses, and silverware he joined the students in their tasks.

The aroma of the cooking quiche was intoxicating. It caused the hunger pangs to rush into awareness. Gerald and some of the students continued their work, cleaning greens for salads at each plate. Lily gave her attention to the preparation of a cake for dessert. The cake would go into the over the moment the quiche was taken out to serve the guests.

Jimmy James was at the door to greet the mayor and members of the city council as they arrived. "Good to see you, mayor. And good to have you here for lunch, all of you. This is a very special gift that Lily Wong gives to this community. Some day you will pay a big price for an elegant dinner prepared by a chef that got his or her start at Lily Wong's Cooking School. But for now be our guests for a delightful meal prepared by the young people; they're the pride of Bloomfield"

With that they were each seated at the table, assisted by a member of the Cooking School. They were served their salads, with a special dressing prepared by the students, assisted by Mrs. Wong. It was all done with the same care anyone would have expected at the finest restaurants in the country. The smiles of appreciation directed to individual students reinforced the students' feeling of self worth.

The aroma of the quiche only anticipated the expectation of what was to follow. A generous portion of quiche was accompanied on the plate by a slice of fresh fruit and buttered string beans. One student brought a basket of rolls which they had baked earlier in the day. Conversations earlier, which had centered around city issues, now quickly shifted to the excellence of the food.

The students listened carefully, noting that what they created was truly valued. "What a great lesson to be learned," Geoffrey thought to himself. "One answer to the earlier questions I asked Mr. Brown. Give of the gift you possess. It will be appreciated. What is the gift each of us may share?"

Lily Wong stood quietly at the door of her kitchen, smiling to herself, at the success her students were enjoying. Geoffrey watched her and knew why she was smiling, and in part why she was doing Lily Wong Cooking School. She thought, "I smell the cake. Better check to see if it is done." Selecting a student, she told him how to check it. In meeting the test, the student removed the cake to allow it to rest before they would cut it, and serve it with a pudding they had prepared that morning.

When they finished the dinner, the mayor rose at his place. "Lily Wong, you and your students are a gift to this community. What you create is far more than the salad, the quiche, and the cake with pudding. You are creating the love of life, and the wonderful ability to give of oneself to others. I am inviting you and your students to attend our Council meeting next Tuesday evening. The city of Bloomfield must know of the gifts each of you possess and share. Thank you very much. We have all been blessed by the sharing of your gifts." The mayor and members of the Council took time to individually shake the hand of each student and to share their appreciation. They left to return to their work for the city.

Gerald James rose from his chair at the side of the room. He had not spoken a word during the lunch, although he did take time to join his father in greeting the guests. "After you have finished your lunch, and I must say how very impressed I am with your work, I would like us to meet for a study session. I know Mr. Gordon and Geoffrey are here to do hair cuts for anyone wanting that. Learning to cook is one thing. If you are going to be the owner of a large restaurant, and I expect some of you will, there is a business issue to be done. I do all the financial work for my father's business, the Supreme Food Products Company. In the weeks to follow I will be inviting you to join me in knowing how to keep the books. While that is not the primary purpose of our work, if we don't attend to it we run the possibility of not achieving our objectives. Enjoy your lunch and be ready to work with a lot of math."

Geoffrey was beginning to see how each part of a system works together to lead to success. It is never just one component of the system. "I'm beginning to see how what Mr. Brown is helping me to see and hear from the barber chair is much like Mrs. Wong's Cooking School, which is much like the system of government headed by the mayor and council. Everything works together. Each part is important but only when it's fully connected to everything else. What happens when things don't work together? What is the price we have to pay?

Gordon and Geoffrey cut the hair of a couple students while Gerald James conducted his class in finance. When it was all done, Gordon and Geoffrey packed up their equipment and headed back to Baronsville.

"You've been very quiet, Geoffrey. What's going through your head?"

"So much to think about. I saw so many great things today. I have a difficult time sorting everything out so I can get to the bigger questions. It's not easy,." Geoffrey answered.

"Keep it all stored in your mind. In time the questions will emerge, and then they will become increasingly important to you. Do not settle on the easy questions. Remember the 'why'. Keep digging deeper with the 'why' questions. They will come."

Not much more was said. Silence was an impressive gift. When they arrived back at the barbershop they unloaded the equipment, and without saying much more, each went his own way in silence.

# CHAPTER 11

## *And at the Diner*

One could almost set their watchers for 6:00 am on Monday morning at Alice's Diner. The gang of guys, as a routine, arrived within minutes of each other. Throwing their hats to see who could best cap the top of the hall tree where coats and hats were hung. It all resulted in a jovial, playful entrance to breakfast.

"Hey, Lily, some of us heard the City Council on the radio last evening. Congratulations on the recognitions which you and your students received," one of the guys called out.

"Musta been quite a shindig. Those kids must be comin' right along," another added.

Billy Burke said, "I really enjoyed the ways those guys and gals work together the day I come up to your school with Gordon and that high school kid he's taken under his wing."

"I heer'd that Mr. James is very impressed with the work you're doin'. Is it true his son is catchin' the fever and starting some business lessons fer the kids?"

"I 'speck some of us could use a little bit of that kinda larnin," one of the new ones to the Monday gang replied.

"We're proud o' yuh, Lily. Now how 'bout two eggs over easy, some grits, and whole wheat toast."

Alice intervened, "Let me take your orders so's we keep the orders straight. Okay, who's first?"

It was only a courtesy, 'cause each always ordered the same thing. Alice had already served each a cup of hot brew, to get their conversation started. When breakfast was finished and all the news or gossip of Baronsville was shared, each paid his check, left a tip for Lily, and headed out for the day's work. While the news of what was happening in Korea was known, it seemed so far removed from life in rural Ohio. Most seemed not to be touched by the news.

# CHAPTER 12

## *At the Roberts*

Jack arrived at home at the usual time, having left school in a hurry. He grabbed the Bloomfield newspaper to get caught up on what was happening in the world.; most of it what was happening on the Korean peninsula.

"Mom, a representative from the armed forces was at school today, inviting us to enlist in one of the services. I can almost taste the power of sitting in a plane and pushing the throttle and surging up into the sky. Wow, what control I'd have. He said we could graduate from high school and then be called into service." Jack came alive in his enthusiasm for what might be ahead for him. "Oh, mom, can't you just picture me in my Air Force uniform, sitting in the pilot seat, and then sweeping upward toward forever? What power! Oh, the importance of being a pilot."

"You are more and more like your father," his mother replied. "I hear how much this appeals to you. I fear for you."

"But, mom, a guy's gotta feel that he's making a difference, that others will want to be a part of his life, wanna share in his ambitions. I don't wanna be stuck in this burg. I wanna go places, do things, be important, make lotsa money!"

"Life is more than money and power, Jack. It's something we all have to learn."

"But, I really like the excitement that comes from being where the action is. And winning is important. That's where I want to be! Where's the excitement in Baronsville?"

Jack didn't want to hear any more. Grabbing his books and materials from school he rushed to his room. "Call me when supper's ready!"

Mitch Roberts did arrive for supper just in time to throw his jacket over a chair and rush to his seat at the table. "What a wonderful day! I had some mind-altering ideas that grew from conversations with clients. My golf game was nothing to talk about, but the ideas on how to make Supreme Food Products lucrative were amazing. I can't wait to tell Mr. James my ideas."

They hadn't seen Mitch so animated for a long time. Excitedly he continued. "When Mr. James sees how much money we can make he'll be overwhelmed. That'll result in his making me president of the company, and then we'll go places. We'll put Baronsville on the map! Baronsville, the home of the Mitch Robert's family!"

Jack continued, "I want out of Baronsville. I can't find much action here. People get excited when I help them win a game.

Otherwise I'm a nobody. A recruiter from the armed forces was at school today. He got me all excited about joinin' the Air Force after I graduate. Dad, can't you jist see me in the cockpit of a fighter plane and goin' fast and goin' way above the clouds? Oh, man, my ticker jist begins pumpin' faster, thinkin' 'bout it."

"Oh, do I know what you're thinking. You wouldn't be a Roberts if you didn't have some of that blood in you. Sometimes we can't get what we want right off, but you keep working at it, and you push forward, sometimes at unbelievable risks. I can't wait to be in charge of creating a powerful company. It's like your surge while piloting a plane. Go after what you want."

Jack didn't dare reveal some of the other things he wanted. Would his parents understand the dreams that he now has about sex with Carrie O'Conner? Certainly his father can remember those times in his life when he experienced those dreams. When he's shared a little of the dreams with the other guys, he found that they, too, had those same kinds of dreams. It must be a part of growing up. But how could going to church and seeing the sun shine on Carries long blond hair have such an intense response? "Go after what you want. Can I?" he thought.

Supper at the Roberts suddenly turned quiet. Jack could not get his images of Carrie out off his mind. Mitch fantasized what his life would be like when he became president of Supreme Food Products Company. And Gladys Roberts wondered how she had come to this point when her ideas were so distant from those of her husband and son.

How could growing up in a town, much like Baronsville, and meeting a dashing young man who visited her town result in her becoming his wife? The courtship had been short. Mitch was so positive. He seemed to have the answer for any question. Like Jack, he was a beautiful, physical young man. He seemed so much more mature than the other boys in her town. He filled her life with invitations. There were those times of talk over cokes at the drug store. Jokes, and idle chatter was playful, and fun. It was a wonderfully exciting time.

And then there was the time when he had his dad's car and they went for a drive. He found a quiet, secluded place and parked the car. Her memories became words. "He put his arms around me and covered me with kisses. I remember the feeling. And then he put his hand on my knee. I can't remember what I did but he became more aggressive, and I felt his hand moving up my leg. I remember I could hardly breathe. Before I could gain my control he had pulled aside my panties and touched me. It all happened so fast, and almost immediately he unzipped his pants and put my hand on his thing. And before I could think straight we had sex. It was both painful and glorious.

A part of me felt a new feeling. It felt good. Another part felt the guilt that came from what was approved of in my town. Sex was something saved for marriage. But, how often was that practiced before a wedding day? How could I have controlled those strong physical feelings that seemed so right in one sense and yet feel the guilt from what had happened?"

As she cleared the table, and did the dishes, she wondered would Jack, so much like his father, struggle with these same human hungers?

Jack and his father left the table tasks to mother and wife, while they retired to the living room to continue their conversations. It was interesting. Each continued to talk about their current interests and passions without seemingly talking with each other.

As his mother entered the room, Jack asked, "Dad, can I borrow the car sometime this weekend. If'n I can get Carrie to join me, I'd like to take her on a picnic and see some of the sights around town. Mom, could you help me prepare some picnic stuff? I'd like it to be very special."

Gladys Roberts thought to herself, "Does history repeat itself? How do we make sure our children are safe?"

Jack had begun his count down. Unsure of just how everything would take place, he4 was following his desires and he would push things to their limits. Now to create an invitation to Carrie, something she might agree to. "I'll pretend to have a party for a group that she'd be willing to join, and then at the last minute they wouldn't be able to come. I would have her alone!" With a smug feeling that he could pull it off he, smiling to himself, excused himself and headed for his room, to his homework and sleep.

The conversation between Gladys and Mitch was sparse. But then that was often the reality. Their lives had taken such different directions. In fact, they probably always had little in common, except for a son.

# CHAPTER 13

## *At Alice's Diner*

Carrie and Geoffrey had made a regular thing of stopping for a coke after school. It was strange that, at times, conversation didn't need to happen. Just being together was what really mattered.

Alice smiled as she observed that Geoffrey no longer sat across the booth from Carrie but that they had managed to sit side by side on one seat in the booth. She smiled, seeing that each time they came for a coke they seemed to sit more closely together. Each time they always chose to sit in the corner booth away from other customers. "Young love is so wonderful!" thought Alice. "No tin roofs and free cokes are needed any longer. I suspect they're getting ready to live on love alone."

"What do you want to do after you graduate from high school, Carrie?" Geoffrey asked.

"I really haven't decided what I want most. I like the creative stuff I've done with my writing in English classes, especially when

Reverend Ryan is substituting. I get turned on when I'm asked to assist with the very young children in the Sunday School classes. I guess that what I'm moving toward is working with people. I just can't decide with what age I want to work. What's in your future, Jeff?"

"I've gained so much in working with Mr. Brown and the things we're doing at Lily Wong's Cooking School. It's the people connection that gives meaning for me. I am thinking that what is important is to support people who face difficult problems, things that weren't in their plan books. Those kids at Lily Wong's Cooking School didn't ask to be poor or any of the other things that determine their lives. I think I'm called to help others face their problems and to help them find their own answers."

"You're wonderful, Geoffrey. I really like what I hear you say. You make it easy for others to trust you. I'm happy to know you. You make our relationship so wonderful."

They moved themselves closer to each other. Geoffrey put his arm around Carrie and drew her to him. Carrie didn't resist but added to the togetherness.

Alice was so wrapped up in her observing the young couple that she didn't notice that the Ryans had come into the diner and had found their seats at a table.

"Is there any service around this place, Alice? What are two hungry people, who have to make an early church meeting, going to do if they can't get fed?"

"Don't give me a bad time, 'preach'. It's all your fault. You had those young people in your Sunday School classes really getting in touch with that stuff about love," Alice spoke quietly. "Can I help it if I get excited when I see love in bloom?" She smiled and nodded her head to the corner booth, and Geoffrey and Carrie.

The Ryans turned, saw the two together, then turned to each other and smiling almost said in unison, "Brings back those days in our togetherness."

Lily's special this night, being Friday, was clam chowder, Lake Erie pike, baked potato, fresh green beans shipped in from Florida, and magnificent home made rolls. Her dessert was her special Amish sour cream pie, rich in taste and calories. It was a recipe she learned from Mr. James' mother. His mother had learned it from her work with the Amish people coming to the area.

The Ryans became fully invested in their food and the service from Alice. They missed seeing Geoffrey and Carrie leave. Alice didn't miss their leaving. She watched them, hand in hand, move to the door. Geoffrey and Carrie dropped hands so that he could open the door for their leaving.

"Oh, what a free coke and a tin roof sundae can do for mankind!" thought Alice. She returned to her work; brought the coffee pot and two cups to the table for the Ryans. "Coffee on the house today, in celebration of young lovers, even when the preacher and his wife are such lovers!"

Grace reached over taking her husband hand in hers and said, "Does it still show?"

"I'm afraid so!" Richard replied, feeling the energy surge through their hands. "How very lucky for me that I found you!"

"Dessert? Amish Sour Cream pie is special"

"Oh, okay. One piece which we can share. Tomorrow? How can I get rid of what I love but don't know how to control?" Grace replied.

"There's a sermon topic there,." Richard added.

Alice brought the pie, two forks and an extra plate. They eagerly consumed their dessert . Paying their bill, they left hand in hand.

"Oh, the power of the Diner and Lily's cooking. It's like four bird caught in one net. But then, love and our coming together is one of the reasons we exist Be sure it is in love!" With that Alice,cleared the table, stuffed the tip in her apron, and went, smilingly, about her work.

# CHAPTER 14

## *At Baronsville High*

"Mornin',Carrie. Great to see you. I was so impressed with the way you read the scriptures the day Reverend Ryan invited Lily and me to be part of his service. That man is something else," Sammy said, as he pushed the broom down the hall, side by side with Carrie.

"You got that right, Sammy." Carried replied. "Your presence there, as here, makes all of us feel better. Thank you." Carrie seemed to stand a little taller as she made her way to her first class of the day. It was her senior English class.

"Reverend Ryan, you're our 'sub' today? How lucky can we be? What great thing is about to happen?" asked Carrie.

"It'll be something that you'll really like, and that I've noticed you do so very well. We're going to create poetry. Does that 'grab' you?' he asked.

"Something new 'bout the way we'll be doing it?" she asked.

"You'll just have to wait and see! Don't we always search for new ways of thinking about things? If you know how to think through something, is it fair just to keep doing it? I don't think so," was his answer. "Oh there's the bell. You better get in your seat 'fore you get trampled by the crowd and they surge in to learn." he added with a knowing smile.

The last student came into the room, closing the door behind him. They all looked at Reverend Ryan, first with surprise and then with a smile of satisfaction and acceptance.

"Good to have you back, Preach," a student said with a sense of playfulness.

"Thank you, George. It's good to be back with all of you. I enjoy the time when I'm called to substitute. Oh, and by the way, George, I prefer to be called Mr. Ryan when I have the opportunity to work with you." Mr. Ryan recorded the attendance and then began the writing activities.

"Previously, we have written poetry that grew from our observations of nature or from those rich, rewarding events in our lives. Those are most important. They help us to become more fully aware of the things that enrich our lives; the things that help us to be more sensitive to others about us, and to the beauty in nature.

Today, I'd like you to think about where there may be struggles, those experiences that do not meet your expectations, or meet you interests. Name what that is and describe how you experience that. Then, pose in your own mind what might be the solutions of the issue. Do you have any questions?"

"Do we put that into some form of poetry? What might it look like? What do you want?" George asked.

"Good question, George. The form is important but having the idea, and beginning to express it, is what is really important. Once your idea begins to take shape, and its function is known, you will probably find that the form will follow. Know what you want to say and then explore how it can best be said. It's not what I want that matters but how you find a way of expressing your feeling," Mr. Ryan added.

"I find it easier if I have a model to begin with," said Betty Baird. "Can you do an example?"

"Many people have problems with trust. Trust might be the topic. An opening line might be: 'How can I learn to trust?' When you think of trusting, when do you trust the most? And when is learning to trust yourself to something, or others difficult?" Mr. Ryan replied.

"I'm learning to trust some people when I feel they're being honest with me," said Carrie. "Trust feels unsure when I think others are after something that is only good for them and not for all that is involved."

Betty added, "I sometimes don't trust myself when I think the teacher has an only answer to the way of doing something. I suppose that's why I asked for an example to follow. So many times there's little freedom in how we get something done."

"How would you complete this line: 'Trust: I can trust when…Or, trust seems to be absent when….'" Mr. Ryan prompted, then continued, "Betty, how would you express your feeling in a few words, and complete this phrase: "How can I trust myself when…'

There is no right or wrong in the process. What is important is that the expressions are honest with you feelings, and hopefully the thoughts have something in common with what others are feeling. Say what you have to say with a minimum of words, words that best express the ideas. Take some time to think about your feelings. Sketch out words around your central idea. Don't worry about putting them into form at the beginning. When your words are there, you'll find the phrases which will contain them. Good writing!"

"It is increasingly difficult to keep a centered on learning or even creating. It is easier to follow the Baltimore Oriole build its low hanging nest in the tree just outside the window of the classroom. Twig by twig she comes and puts the twigs in place until it is hanging low. What amazing skill and precision!. It seemed to be at a frantic pace, the need to be ready for the depositing of the eggs and the birthing of the chirping wonders," George observed.

"That's very poetic, the way you described it," Mr. Ryan replied.

The class period with Mr. Ryan went too fast. Geoffrey observed that almost every student became involved, everyone except Jack. Jack seemed in a world of his own. What was he thinking about? Would it be something that he could share with others in the class?

In the end, Jack had not finished his writing. He left without saying a word to anyone.

There were only weeks before the graduation and the separation into new experiences, and new relationships. The principal had called Carrie to his office to tell her the faculty had decided she would be invited to present the Senior Class speech at the graduation services. Carrie's grades were the highest and the faculty was most impressed by her leadership in the school.

Carrie was, to put it mildly,'bowled over'. "What in the world will I have to say?" she thought to herself. "It's a wonderful opportunity! But how do I begin to put my ideas together? There are others who are more comfortable in speaking? All at once, I'm feeling excitement to do what is asked of me, and at the same time, terror."

Three weeks until graduation! Night after night Carrie would awaken from her sleep to search for an answer to her invitation. Nothing would come! There were no answers! As the days wore on, the search for ideas filled her thoughts.

It was only two weeks away when Carrie awakened early with the title of her speech fixed in her mind: Hold On To Dreams. "I need to become aware of my true dreams and then to do those things that help me realize them. But isn't that what each person is called to do? How can I reflect the truth of that search in a way that means something to others? And what do we do when things get in our way, or interrupt our dreams? And how do we hold on to dreams when new things enter our lives? I can't wait to talk with Geoffrey about the topic. Maybe we can go to Alice's Diner after school to talk it over."

Carrie dressed and joined her mother and father for breakfast.

"Now tell us what's happening. You seem more relaxed and excited than we've seen you in the last week," her mother observed.

"Is it something new with Geoffrey?" asked her father.

"Oh, Daddy! Remember, I told you that the principal had invited me to give the valedictorian address at the graduation services. I've really struggled this past week, trying to think about what I have to say, or want to say. I stayed awake at night trying to find a topic. I couldn't find it. In my half-dream this morning, the title came to me. It is "Hold On to Dreams" What does that title mean to you?"

"That has the potential of pretty deep thoughts, young lady," replied her father. "I sometimes am not aware that I have dreams, but something inside me seems to help me make choices that keep things working for us. Is that a part of what you're thinking?"

Carrie's mother added, "All my dreams were very simple, yet at times they seemed difficult and hard to hold on to. For the most part I have been very blessed. That's not to say that I haven't had times when it was easy. My life with my parents and friends was wonderful, so wonderful that my dream was to find a life like I had observed and lived. I dreamed of being married and having a wonderful family. Then I met your father and my dream began to take shape. You have been a wonderful part of my dream."

"How can a girl be so lucky to have been born into a family like mine. It's so easy to know love. I suspect that that's much of what I will have to say."

Marty O'Connor served breakfast, and the father shared a blessing," Oh, gracious Lord, we give thanks for this day, the love shared, and the food prepared for us. For the invitations to living, we are most grateful. In your holy name, Amen."

Was it the special touch of Marty's cooking, or the renewed awareness of love that made the bacon, poached eggs, and toast, taste so good?

They completed breakfast. Marty cleared the table, washed, and dried the dishes. Craig completed his morning rituals of shaving, and combing his hair, before leaving for work. Carrie excitedly prepared for school. "I can't wait to see Geoffrey to share the ideas," she thought to herself.

Carrie almost danced her way to school.

"Well, I do believe that I see a young lady about to take off and fly. Mornin', Carrie. What's happenin'? Oh, and by the way, congratulations on being selected to give the valedictorian talk at the commencement program. The faculty is most positive about the invitation. I'm really pleased, too," Sammy said with his customary warm greeting.

"Oh, Sammy, or should I say, Mr. Brown?"

"Make it Sammy. Mr. Brown sounds too formal. Sammy feels friendlier!"

Carrie continued, "I really spent a wild time last week. I couldn't think of what I have to say or need to say. In some way, I imagine that people will expect me to speak for all the youth in our graduating class. That's a big order. This morning I found a title. It's 'Hold on to Dreams.' I'll be coming to find out what that means to you. I keep wondering what that title means to many people who live or work in Baronsville. Thanks, Sammy, for being so aware of each of us."

Just then Geoffrey came through the hall, quickly greeted Sammy before giving his full attention to Carrie.

She interrupted his expected words. "Geoffrey, can we stop at Alice's Diner after school? I have so much to tell you, and my parents gave me my weekly allowance, so it's my turn to buy the cokes."

Geoffrey was unsure of what was going to happen, but pleased to see Carrie filled with so much excitement. "How can a guy turn down an offer like that? If he did, he ought to have his head examined."

The bell rang, and they hurried off to their first period class.

The day seemed to last forever. Carrie could hardly wait to share with Geoffrey her thinking since early this morning. Spending time with Geoffrey had become an increasingly important activity in Carrie's life.

The last bell of the day had rung. Students rushed from the building. Carrie and Geoffrey waited a brief time so they could quietly and silently leave the building together. Without any delay they made their way to Alice's Diner.

As they burst into the Diner, Alice greeted them saying,"Well, what's happening? Ain't seen such excitement in a long time!"

"I don't know what's happening. Carrie's all excited about somethin'. She said she wasn't gonna tell me until we got to Alice's Diner. Is there some kinda magic in this place?"

Carrie then said, "What a silly question! His memory must be getting' shot. I guess he can't remember what's been happening every time we come for a coke!"

"Well, I guess that calls for a couple of cokes, on the house," Alice added, and Carrie and Geoffrey found their place side by side in their corner booth. Alice returned quickly with two cokes and a piece of Lily's delicious dessert, a piece of double chocolate cake. "Whatever it is, it will need feeding." With a big, knowing smile, Alice returned to her work.

There was a moment of silence as Geoffrey waited for Carrie to share her excitement.

"Geoffrey, I'm sure you've heard that the faculty invited me to give the talk for the class at our graduation exercises." Geoffrey nodded that he knew. "I've had a terrible week trying to decide what I wanted and needed to say. I'd lay awake at night trying to find a topic. But nothing same."

"I didn't know what was happening, but I was aware that something was wrong. Everyone in our class now knows. Almost everyone is very pleased. I'm so proud of you. I know what you will say will be great," Geoffrey added.

"Well, this morning, as I was getting awake, and half in dreams, the thought of a topic came to me. It was 'Hang on to Dreams'. When I shared it with my parents, they were most positive and shared a bit of their dreams they have held, and how it has made a difference in our lives together. What they had to say, is a part of who I am. My dreams are taking shape. You have contributed to those dreams. I have much yet to think through as I decide what I want for my life."

"Wow! That's a heavy! I often think about how the people in my life have helped me shape my dreams," Geoffrey added. "The Sunday School class at church, and the leadership of Mr. Brown, has been very helpful. Our visiting Lily Wong's Cooking School made me think about who I wanted to work with. I saw that people giving of their gifts made a difference in the lives of others. My dream is to somehow work with people."

"I've watched that happen with you, and as that began to happen you were someone I needed to know more. Then there was the first time here at the Diner. You gave me such positive responses to my reading of the scriptures at church that I was aware I wished to trust you and to know you even more," Carrie continued. "Then I remember the moment you reached across the table and took my hand as we continued talking, that I found my dreams beginning to happen."

"That happened for me, too. Do you remember the time after our cokes here that I walked you home. We tried to be casual,.not let anyone know what was beginning to happen. You told me your parents saw through it all. We were found out! Now, a dream I have is that you are a part of my life. I can't imagine anything happening that would change the way I feel about you." Geoffrey spoke in almost a whisper but with firmness, as he reached out to once more take Carrie's hand.

"One of my dreams,"Carrie began, "is that I think I'd like to be a writer. There is so much good in Baronsville that needs to be told. When Reverend Ryan has substituted in our English classes and invited us to write, that's been a biggie. Imagine telling stories of the little events in life that people give that make such a difference. That was what Reverend Ryan was telling us the day the gong and the cymbals were a part of the church service and he introduced Lily Wong and Sammy to the members of our church. I don't fully understand it, but there is something about the beauty and truth in everything we do, if we but search for it."

"How are you going to learn about the dreams of others and the part their dreams play in their lives?" Geoffrey asked.

"Reverend Ryan has played an important part in my interests, and dreams. I'd like to know how his dreams and his marriage have filled his dreams," Carrie said. "I'm gonna call him tonight and see if I could talk with him and Mrs. Ryan."

The exchange felt relatively complete. They went to Alice. "Thank you, Alice. I was gonna treat Geoffrey today. But thank you. We talked about dreams and holding on to one's dreams. I'd like to find a time when I could talk to you about your dreams."

"Thank you, Carrie. I'd like that. Having to think about that would probably be very helpful to me in finding my way in Baronsville," Alice replied.

Geoffrey opened the door as they stepped out into the warm afternoon sunshine. The air seemed more velvety and enveloping as Geoffrey walked Carrie to her house.

There was another moment of silence and awkwardness as they reached Carrie's front door. She looked into his eyes as he bent over and kissed her forehead.

"Is that all there'll be," Carrie said teasingly.

"You asked for it," he replied playfully, as he reached once more and kissed her on the lips.

Carrie blushed her crimson best as Geoffrey rushed for home, hoping no-one would see the deep joy that filled his body.

Carrie rushed inside, stacking her books on the coffee table in the living room. "I gotta call Reverend Ryan and see if I can meet him and his wife after school tomorrow."

Marty encouraged Carrie, "Go for it! You know how to dial his number. Probably Mrs. Ryan is home, if he's not."

Carrie picked up the phone and dialed the Ryan's number.

"This is the Ryan home," Mr. Ryan said, answering her call. "My I help you?"

"This is Carrie O'Conner. I've been invited to give the talk at our graduation services at school. I'd like to talk with you and Mrs. Ryan about my topic. Could I meet at Alice's Diner tomorrow after school?"

"I have a better idea. I'm substituting tomorrow. Could we meet in the choral music room with Mrs. Ryan after the bell rings? All three of us are very close to her room."

"Thanks, Mr. Ryan. I like that idea,." Carrie replied. "Thank you for the suggestion,." she said putting the phone in its cradle.

The end of the day school bell rang. Carrie gathered her homework together and headed for the choral room. She arrived moments before Mr. Ryan.

"Oh, I love this place. I have such good, warm memories of what we create together. I can close my eyes and almost hear the sound of the music. Every object in the room seems to come alive with memories," Carrie said, closing her eyes and standing quietly and facing the area where the singers sit, as if to hear the tones more clearly.

"Come back, Carrie. You had something you wanted to talk about with Mrs. Ryan and myself?" Reverend Ryan asked.

"I'm sorry. This room holds so many memories for me. I've been invited to give the graduation address this year. Yesterday, as I awakened, I found a working title. It's 'Hold On to Dreams.'. Does that have any special meaning for Mrs. Ryan and you?"

"I'll begin," said Grace Ryan. "Even as a little girl, music was so wonderful for me. I could easily get caught up in the excitement of the sounds. I was very young when I started piano lessons. I loved to touch the piano keys and listen to the magic. In high school I was involved in every music activity I could find. I wanted to be a music teacher. That was my dream."

"My dream involved drama. My parents loved theater and we saw as many plays as we could afford. I wanted to be an actor. I auditioned for every play I could. I loved the sound of applause, and the praise I got for my acting. I dreamed of seeing my name in lights in the theaters in New York City. I continued that dream in college. Then there came the realization that one had to be very excellent to make the big time."

"So what did you do?" asked Carrie.

"I decided that, being a teacher, I could still find the dream within plays, but I'd be sure of a job and something for my table. I became a teacher. Miss Smith was the choral music teacher in the first school where I taught English and Drama. A friend gave me two tickets to a production that arrived on tour. I looked for someone who might accompany me to that play. Miss Grace Smith happened to have lunch in the faculty dining room at the very moment I was there and we sat opposite each other.

I'll bet you can guess what happened next. I said,.' I have two tickets for tonight for the play in town. I apologize for such a late invitation but would you like to go?"

"Would I? What a silly question,." Grace added. "What young single lady wouldn't have noticed the new English-Drama teacher in the school? I added, 'I think I can arrange to be available!'"

"You probably know what happened then. There were more plays, and concerts to attend. Miss Smith became Mrs. Ryan. And then there came the moment when I received the call to go into the ministry.," Mr. Ryan added. "Our dreams seemed to come together. My passion for the theater was not lost when I became a minister. In fact each of our dreams seemed to become greater. I find to create drama in the midst of church services makes things seem more real."

"One of those dramas was the Sunday you based the service on First Corinthian Chapter 13. The drama of that service had a great impact on members of the church. You took an ordinary experience and made it special," Carrie said. "Your being together and following your dreams was somehow made more special.

Thank you, both, for sharing your dreams and holding them." Carrie picked up her homework and her books to head for home.

As she prepared to leave Carrie added, "When you introduced Sammy and Lily Wong you made their work a very special gift. I must learn the dreams they hold. I must talk with Sammy tomorrow, if he's available. I can't wait to tell Geoffrey about what I'm learning."

# CHAPTER 15

## *At Baronsville High*

Early the next morning Carrie head for the high school, hoping to catch Sammy before his work swallowed up his time. She found him resting on a bench in the furnace room.

"May I ask you some questions, Sammy?"

"I best come out where we can talk," Sammy replied. "Now how can I help, Miss Carrie?"

"I'm to do the valedictorian talk at our graduation,." Carrie said. "I've chosen a title 'Hold On To Dreams'., and I'm interested in what that title means to you. Could you share your thoughts?"

"You're asking a black man to talk about his dreams? Our people have held to dreams for many years, trusting that right will come our way."

"By the way, Sammy, where did you get the name of Brown," Carrie asked.

"My great grandfather was owned by a gentleman by the name of Josiah Brown. My great grandfather was called Brownsman. In the years that followed, the "man" was dropped and we became known as the 'Brown' family"

"Thanks, Sammy. Oh, back to the dreams."

"As I started to say, our people have dreamed of a day when we could be totally free, to work, play and live that freedom. I love my job here at Baronsville High 'cause you kids treat me like one of you. I love your comin' to me for advice. I regret that I must live in Bloomfield and drive here every day to work. I hold to the dream that someday I can live here and be a part of this place I've learned to love."

Carrie moved closer to Sammy, reaching out to touch his brawny arm. "Thank you, Sammy, for being so special."

School was beginning to be more important. Everything they experienced seemed to suddenly become a part of life. Learning was becoming relevant to life itself. She thought, "If I'm to be a part of life, and to share the beauty in the simple things of life, then I must learn to write. I will register at Bloomfield Community College, just as soon as the summer classes begin. I'm sure they'll have some writing classes."

Carrie hurried on to Alice's Diner the moment the school day ended. When she arrived there was not a soul in the restaurant. "Can I talk with you and Mrs. Wong, Alice? Remember, I'm collecting stories of people's dreams. You and Mrs. Wong are so special. Your dreams come together to make this Diner important to all of us."

"May I talk with you and Mrs. Wong!" Alice called, "Lily, can you come out and answer some questions for Carrie O'Conner. She's givin' the valedictorian talk at their graduation."

Lily came quietly to the table where Alice and Carrie had perched themselves. She pulled out a chair and joined the two. "Yes? What do you want to know?"

"What dreams brought you to Alice's Diner, and to the forming of the Lily Wong's Cooking School? My talk at graduation is about the theme 'Hold on to Dreams'. I'm fascinated by the dreams we each have and how they become a part of each of us. Is there something that happens between the dreams you and Alice hold that makes this place so special?"

Lily began, "Many of my people were brought here as cheap labor. They helped build railroads and much of what brought this part of the country and the west together. My great grandfather and my grandfather had special skills in cooking for the crews at work. They had to create great feasts from the most ordinary things. When the railroads were completed, they hopped aboard a train and headed east. We're not sure why they ended up in Bloomfield, but it's been home for all my life. Their love of food, and making it special, has been a part of all of our lives."

Alice added, "It was my mother that loved to cook. We lived on a farm. During the depression we had all the food we needed or wanted. In the summer during thrashing season, as the thrashing machines moved from farm to farm, the women of the community held an unspoken game of who could create the best dinner for the hungry men who worked the fields. There was always the most hearty meals set on the table. Elegant pies to top off each meal was the order. I was impressed with the praise the women received for the excellence of the prepared meals. Then I went to a little restaurant in Bloomfield and had this great meal. I said I wanted to meet a cook who could prepare a meal as elegant as my mother's. I met Lily. My dream became Alice's Diner. It has become a dream greater than I could have imagined."

"That's true for me, as well," Lily said. "I never knew I would be starting a cooking school. I saw the youth in my neighborhood. They needed a purpose in their lives. I was also aware that restaurants needed chefs to staff their restaurants. I needed something for my time away from Alice's Diner. The Cooking School became a part of my dream."

"I must not take more of your time. You have both been very helpful. Thank you."

Carrie was beginning to grasp the important factors in her theme. She raced home to locate some paper and a pencil to begin writing the valedictorian talk. Words flowed, almost without end. Ideas rushed through her mind and quickly found their place on the paper.

At last the speech was completed. She decided to secretly hold the words until the night of the graduation. Not even would she share them with Geoffrey. She would not tell her parents about what she had prepared. Part of the purpose of writing and speaking is to prepare the reader or listener to follow one's thoughts, but to keep some elements of surprise to hold their interests. Most people would know by now that she had been interviewing people in the Baronsville community. Notice of what is happening is usually known by everyone.

The last Wednesday of the school year had arrived. The band had diligently practiced the processional music, Elgar's "Pomp and Circumstance." The gymnasium had been transformed into a crepe paper fairyland. Peonies from local gardens had been cut and set out in their brilliant colors at the front of the stage. Some potted green plants from a Bloomfield nursery completed the front of the stage. Chairs had been placed on the stage for those that were to be a part of the program. Twenty four chairs had been roped off at the front of the audience for the members of the graduating class. Carrie was to sit on the stage,

At last the evening had come. People arrived to celebrate that which was to become a new beginning for the twenty-five graduating seniors. The chevys and fords filled a part of the baseball field. Mr. and Mrs. Roberts and their son Jack arrived in Mr. Roberts' new Lincoln. He parked it right in front of the school that all might witness his presence.

The chatter among the people was suddenly interrupted by the music from the band; "Pomp and Circumstance." The class walked slowly in pairs to their seats at the front of the hall, They were followed by the superintendent and the principal, Reverend Ryan, and Carrie.

When the band sounded the last chord, Superintendent Frye rose from his chair and walked to the podium. "Welcome to this evening of beginnings. Our community is blessed with the work of these young people. They have shown unusual interest in that which makes the community of Baronsville the wonderful place it is. We will be even more blessed with these young people as they join us in coming together to extend the needs before us. Will you welcome, please, our principal of Baronsville High, Mr. Jason Wright. Mr. Wright."

Applause followed, as Mr. Wright walked to the podium. "Would you stand as the Reverend Ryan leads us in an invocation."

"Creator of all people and all things, we give thanks for the joys and promise of these young people. Guide them in their journey into the future. Help them to find and engage the best that life has to offer. May they find true joy in love and service to this community, and to all they are invited to serve. We ask these things in Your Holy name. Amen." With that brief prayer, Reverend returned to his seat.

Mr. Wright continued the commentary. "One very special student, Miss Carrie O'Conner, was chosen, by the faculty, to speak for the graduating seniors. Her grades and her leadership0 has been outstanding. She would probably think that others are more worthy. It is this quality and the depth of her search in learning that resulted in the unanimous choice of our teachers. Welcome, please, Miss Carrie O'Conner. Carrie".

With exemplary dignity Carrie rose from her seat, with her written speech in hand, and stood behind the podium. She paused for a moment before beginning, as if to collect her breath, her composure, and her thoughts. Scanning the audience, she began:

"It was but just weeks ago that Mr. Wright asked me to his office to invite me to this moment. A part of me was terrified. What would I say? What did I have to say? What is important for us to think about as we begin a new phase of our lives. For more than a week, I struggled to find a topic for what I wanted to say. Nothing came to me. Night after night I would lie awake trying to find an answer. Than one morning, when I was half awake and half asleep, I heard the words: "Hold On To Dreams'.

What does Holding on to Dreams have to do with a graduating senior? What does it have to do with all of us in this community, or any community? What does it have to do with life?

Where would I find the answers to my questions? When we were eating breakfast I asked by parents what the title 'Hold On to Dreams' meant to them. My father made a wise answer, "I don't know that I've ever thought about my dreams, but there's something inside of me that guides my choices and makes for a wonderful life together as a family

I would guess that that is true for many of us. We haven't ever put into a thought our individual dreams, but there are values we hold that constantly guide our choices.

Mr mother talked about her life as a child, and the richness of those relationships with her parent sand friends. They were so powerful that, as she become an adult, she wanted to provide that for those that were a part of her life. I have benefited greatly from that dream. That is probably true for many people in this audience this evening.

I consulted a classmate about the meaning of the title, as he thought about it. He was mostly aware of how his dream was being shaped by the quality of those special relationships in his life." Geoffrey looked up to Carrie from his seat in the front row of the audience, and winked. "In a very real sense, that was true in every discussion I had. I expect that is true for most, if not all of you,

Reverend and Grace Ryan shared their dreams for music, and acting. When they found each other, their dreams persisted and became ever greater. Then Mr. Ryan, a teacher of English and drama, received a call to the ministry. Their dreams fit into their expanded service to the community. Reverend Ryan found his thirst for drama to be an important part of worship and his ministry. He confessed, that within the scriptures, there is incredible drama. Many of us know the effect, as we have explored the drama of his worship.

I also talked with Alice and Lily at Alice's Diner. Each of them found satisfaction in relationships that were connected with food. By coincidence they found each other through food; food Lily prepared and which Alice enjoyed. Together they have made the Diner a place of small wonders. Lily's Cooking School is increasingly important to the community of Bloomfield. Who knows what the limits of life are, if we but work together?

And Sammy Brown, who the students of Baronsville High love because he first loved us. Sammy's heritage and the long struggle, a part of his people's history, is yet to be fully realized. Sammy Brown holds on to his dream. I'm here to honor him for his persistence in holding to his dream.

So where did the answers to the question of the title of my talk find their answer? It has been a part of our days, each day of our life. Too often they become so much a part of each day's routine that we fail to recognize the power within how we live. Where did I find the answer to my questions? It was right here all the time. Each of you make choices that reflect your dreams. We have but to reach out to each other, celebrate what we have, and work together to realize our dreams. Hold on to dreams!"

Carrie returned to her seat as the whole audience rose up in great applause. A tear dropped from Geoffrey's eyes. Mrs. and Mrs. O'Conner looked at each other, smiling while holding back their tears. Everyone was in awe. One person was heard saying, "I hear she wants to be a writer. With thoughts like that she'll do well!"

The Certificates of Graduation were given to students. Jack thought to himself, as he passed by Carrie, "Hold on to dreams? Oh, that I could!"

Reverend Ryan proceeded to the podium, raised his hands and everyone stood, and he said, "For the wisdom of youth we are most blessed. May this day, and the thoughts expressed, remain with us always. Now, may the blessing of all good and love be with you this day and always."

There was a new sense of presence among the people as they greeted each in leaving. Carrie had touched the soul of so many. They became aware that the smallest of gifts can have the most profound consequences.

Carrie met her parents and Geoffrey together as they prepared to leave. Without an ounce of embarrassment, Geoffrey took Carrie within his arms, and planted a kiss on her forehead. In a hushed tone, and with a wink, Carrie said, "Is that all there is?" That resulted in a shy smile from the man of her dreams.

Graduation of the Barronsille High School class of '48 was history.

# SUMMER

Summer doesn't officially begin until later. There is a clear definition of "summer" as the work on the farm surrounding the village that must be attended. Older youth perform many functions during this time. In a sense, summer has begun with the closing of school.

Summer is a time of testing. Things are measured by what develops, by how they meet established expectations. Corn must be knee high by the Fourth of July? Lawns must be mowed and trimmed to show their beauty. Weeds fed by the summer rain must be given their due. Heat from the summer's long days become refreshing with the advent of a cool summer rain.

Flowers are in full bloom. Even wild flowers lift their heads and cry for recognition. Streams tumble along their routes of least resistance. Gone are the morel mushrooms that once found their place in a cool wooded area. Now, only the memory of their buttery fried taste remains, and the deep desire to await their return at the beginning of summer next year.

Flies? Did we say flies? From where did they come? A moist cow pile in the meadow? How disgusting! And those mosquitoes, what is an evening without having to brush away mosquitoes? And heat? Where can one find a nice cool shaded area?

But then there are the quiet early morning times when all is still. Only the call of a bird announces the day. The call from another bird from the distance seems to say, "I hear you, we're ready for the day!"

The cows in the pasture, awaiting their turn to give milk, lay lazily in the meadow, chewing their cud. Oh, but the grass is so tasty. A young colt dances about its mother as if anticipating a great life ahead. Its mother remembers an earlier time when she was essential to the work on the farm. Now replaced by a tractor and the smell of gas, she, with all about her, wonders about what might take place. What does the summer spell? What will summer bring?

# CHAPTER 16

## *After Graduation*

Sleep came easily for Carrie following the graduation program. Only the bright morning sunlight and the ringing of the telephone interrupted her sleep.

Her mother called, "Carrie, the phone is for you. I think you might like to take it. It's Geoffrey."

"Okay, mom." Carrie pushed back the light covers that encased her. "Tell Geoffrey I'll call him back. Don't tell him I'm not up yet!"

"Geoffrey, Carrie will call you back. It shouldn't be too long. By the way, I was so impressed with you students at your graduation last evening. Thanks for all the support you give to Carrie."

"No, thank you, Mrs. O'Conner. All the students are grateful for the support parents have given to us. Tell Carrie I'll meet her at Alice's Diner as soon as she's able. I'm heading out now."

"Geoffrey's gone on to Alice's Diner, said he'll meet you there as soon as you're able. He's gone on."

"What's so important? I haven't even had breakfast. It's only nine! Only nine? How could I have slept so long?" She rushed to the bathroom, brushed her teeth and combed her hair, then quickly dressed herself. "What does Geoffrey have to say that couldn't wait until later?" She grabbed a slice of toast her mother had made, as she raced out the front door and down the street to the Diner.

Carrie stopped at the door for a moment, took several deep breaths, brushed herself to look composed, as she opened the door and slowly moved to the corner booth where Geoffrey sat waiting.

"Good night's sleep? Bet getting up was a little difficult this morning!" Geoffrey added.

"Does it show?" thought Carrie. "How does he know so much about me without my telling him anything? Can't a young girl keep any secrets to herself?"

"I just had to tell you how important your talk was last evening. I felt the meaning of the dreams that are happening between us."

"I know, Geoffrey. I saw the wink! That felt good," Carrie replied.

"All night long I'd awaken from my sleep to think about us, how important you are becoming in my life. I have the feeling, often, that nothing can come between us." He reached out, taking Carrie's hand, then moving closer to her. Feeling that the intent of his thought had been conveyed, he confessed. "I overslept, too. I didn't take time for breakfast. I'm starving, and, if I know you, you haven't eaten either."

"Yes, Geoffrey,. As always, you're right. Oops! That's a dangerous reply to a guy, always thinking they're right. Betcha guys make mistakes, too. I'm hungry. Wonder what Lily's got cooked up on Thursday morning?"

Geoffrey took charge. "Alice, what's Lily got prepared for two hungry pups that have left school to take up their learnin'?"

"I didn't want to interrupt an early important meeting, you're having settled in that corner booth and bein' aware that something of vast importance must be taking place this early in the mornin'. Don't see many teenagers here this early." Alice stopped for a moment before continuing, time to let her thoughts reach the two graduates. "I think it most appropriate that the Diner treat you both to a a post-graduate experience. Omelets on the house. What'll you have to drink?"

"How about a glass of that cow juice?" Carrie playfully said.

"Make that two," Geoffrey added. "And I'd like some whole wheat toast with mine."

"I'll make that two,to you two, too!" Alice replied, playing the game.

Carrie and Geoffrey loved the playful time they were having with Alice. "This Diner has become a very important place. Oh, if only all of life could be so much fun?" they thought, and seemed to share without having said a word to each other.

Lily looked out at the young couple as she cracked the eggs, whipped them, and poured them into her omelet skillet. She smiled at the potential that a few eggs, cheese, bacon and mushroom can have on a relationship. The omelet, .lightly browned, was rolled onto a plate, dressed with slices of oranges, and a sprig of greens, as a garnish. Lily picked up the two plates and personally brought them to the booth. "Thank you, Carrie, for your thoughts last evening. I was very moved by what you had to say. You helped me get more in touch with the things that matter most in my life." Without waiting for a reply, Lily returned to her place in the kitchen, and to the preparation of meals for other customers.

"How very meaningful! Lily served us herself. But that is the very thing you talked about last evening, the way we really become a family. Thank you, Carrie. See, even the smallest things we do for each other, have such importance in our lives," Geoffrey observed.

The omelets became history. Everything was as it should be, except the burps! They thanked Alice, then hand in hand they made it outside. When they reached the sidewalk, they both stopped for a moment, looking up at the small puffs of clouds above, drinking in the fresh smell of the early perfumed summer air, began their walk to the O'Conner home. Little was said, or needed to be said, for they were so attuned to each other. "If only all people could learn to know each other as we know each other," thought Carrie.

Too soon they seemed to arrived at Carrie's house. "If only life could go on like this forever," they thought without saying a word. At the front door, holding hands as if never wanting to let go, Geoffrey took Carrie in his arms in a warm embrace, then with a gentle kiss, released her to her family, as he went almost floating to his home. "How can trust become so high?"

The euphoria was interrupted by the telephone. "It's for you, Carrie. Must be quite impressive to be so popular after one speech!" her mother said in loving appreciation. "I think it's Jack Roberts."

"What in the world does he want? I thought he was going into service? He wants to be a pilot!. Oh, alright, I'll take it. Hello, this is Carrie."

"Carrie, my mother is preparing picnic for a group as a part of my going away to service. I was hoping you could be part of the picnic. I leave for service next Thursday. My mom is making food for the picnic on Wednesday. I could come by and pick you up a little before noon and we could meet the others at the picnic grounds. Could you come?. It would mean so much to me." Jack said, not giving Carrie time to think or ask questions.

"Well," and with a pause, "I suppose I could go. I have much that I want to get done to explore my dream of becoming a writer."

"Good! I'll pick you up about 11:30 on Wednesday.," and Jack hung up the phone.

"Mom, I'm a little uncomfortable with that call from Jack Roberts, and I don't know why. Since he's going into service, I suppose I should join the rest of our gang who's going to see him off."

"I haven't gotten to know Jack much. But I do like his mother. She seems like she's really a part of Baronsville. I don't think I've ever seen his father. He must be a very busy man," her mother said.

# CHAPTER 17

## *At the Roberts*

"Gladys, did you see the Bloomfield News?" Mitch could hardly contain himself. "It says here that Walter Jordan, president of Supreme Food Products, is retiring on July first. Jim James, owner of the family company is interviewing individuals for the position of president. This is my chance. It's what I've been working for. It's the dream of my life. I must give him a call to get an appointment."

"Yes, Mitch, I wish you well," Gladys replied, knowing that her thoughts mattered little.

Mitch eagerly drew the phone to him as he dialed the Supreme Food Product's phone number.

"Supreme Food Products Company. May I help you?" the voice asked.

"I'd like to talk with Mr. James. Is he in?"

"He's out of the office. Perhaps his secretary can help you. I'm ringing her office."

"Hello, this is Mr. James' office. May I help you?" the secretary asked.

"This is Mitchell Roberts, vice president for marketing for the company. I'd like to have an appointment with Mr. James at his earliest convenience. Tell me your name again. I don't think we've met."

"I'm Miss Franks. Yes, we met once at a party for the company. Oh, Mr. James has an opening on Wednesday afternoon. Could you be available sometime between three and four on Wednesday afternoon?"

"Thank you. I'll be there." A smile of expectant satisfaction filled his face. Then to his wife, "Next Wednesday afternoon. Then Mrs. Roberts, you'll be sleeping with the president of Supreme Foods. We'll make it go places!"

The days bore on. Imaginations were abundant. Everyone in the Roberts' family thought expectantly of what could well be in store.

On the following Wednesday, Mitch Roberts put a little extra after-shave on his cheeks, brushed each hair to a more perfect place on his head, made sure he had chosen the most executive looking tie to adorn his front, and dressed in his finest suit, he headed out the door, without saying goodbye to his wife or son.

Jack could barely contain his excitement. He had dreamed of the possibilities of this day far too often. He put much more aftershave on his face, donned his most casual shirt and pants, then headed down to the kitchen to help his mother make the sandwiches, pack the potato chips and the drinks.

"What's all the excitement, Jack? It's like you're headed for Cedar Point and rides on the roller coaster!. Or is it something even more exciting?" his mother asked.

"Can't share that now, mother. I hope it is more exciting... I don't know how to express it."

Nine, ten, and at last eleven o'clock. Jack grabbed a blanket to spread on the grass for a place for food, and to have the picnic. Just before eleven thirty, Jack loaded all the gear into the car and set off to the O'Conner home. When he arrived he rushed to the door and knocked.

Carrie answered the door. "Are you ready?" he asked.

Looking out to the car, "Where's the rest of the gang?" She asked.

"They'll have to get there on their own. Let's roll. I'm hungry!" Jack let Carrie into the car and closing the door, hurried to his driver's seat. He drove to a secluded place by a stream that cut its way through the meadow. Trees secluded the space.

"How will the others ever find this place, Jack?" as Jack spread the blanket and placed the small basket at one corner of the blanket. "Who else is coming, Jack? Is this a study of the loaves and fishes," she asked looking at the small amount of food and the small basket. Carrie began to feel uncomfortable. "What's happening?" she thought to herself.

Jack moved close to Carrie. "When you talked last week at our graduation, you said 'Hold on to dreams': I have dreamed of you even before I saw you that first Sunday at church when they played the gong and the cymbals, and you read from the bible." He moved even closer and, putting his hands on her shoulders,. pushed her down on the blanket. Night after night I have dreamed of you." He seemed possessed, unable to be aware of Carrie's struggle.

Carrie couldn't believe what was happening. She was becoming frightened. Her whole body became rigid with fright. She could hardly breathe. "Please, Jack, stop it." Tears were streaming down her cheeks. She fought to free herself from his grip. When he tried to kiss her, she quickly turned her head to avoid him. She tightly closed her eyes as if trying to shut out what was happening.

He only pressed on, moving his body to hers. "No, Jack, no! Please don't do this. It's not right."

She heard the sound of a zipper. Jack held her under his grasp. "Carrie, I'm following my dream!" Then she felt his rigid man thing on her leg. She was sobbing loudly. Jack kept pushing up against her body as he reached upward with his body. He began breathing heavily, frantically pursuing his needs. Suddenly his body began an inward shutter, a tightening of the mid-section of his body, a loud exhaling of his breath, and then a sudden release. "I'm sorry, Carrie. I'm sorry!"

Between her sobs, Carrie cried out, "Jack, what have you done? It's such a mess!. Let me up! I want out of here!"

"I'm sorry, Carrie. I'll take you home!"

"I don't want anything from you. .I'll find my own way home." Tears streamed down her cheeks. Her eyes burned with tears. "You lied to me! You never planned a picnic with all the gang from church. I' ll never trust you again! I've never hated anyone before. You've now…." and, with that, Carrie, got up from her place on the blanket, sobbing from deep within, she began her walk home.

When she got to a place where she was alone, she removed her panties and wiped away the sticky mess. When she had finished, she threw her panties behind a bush, next to the stream.

The walk home was horrible. Her thoughts varied from disgust, to anger, to deep disappointment that anyone could be so thoughtless.

When she arrived home, she opened the door and ran to her room, crying as she went. She closed the door to her room and threw herself upon her bed.

"Carrie, are you alright?" No answer. "Carrie, this is your mother. Are you alright?"

"I want to be left alone!" she uttered between sobs. "I can't talk about it. It was so awful!"

"Please let me in. I want to help you."

"Go away! I'll talk with you later! Right now I want to be alone. I don't want to see anyone. I have to have time to think."

"Alright, honey, I'll be here when you want me." Marty O'Conner quietly walked down the stairs to the kitchen where she was finishing the washing of the dishes from lunch. "I wonder if Carrie had anything to eat,. I've never seen her in such a state. "Then she added to her thoughts, "Now, Marty, she's a young lady. She'll come to you when she wants and needs you!"

Jack picked up the basket of food, folded the blanket, used a napkin to clean himself, then putting the things in his car, began his trip home. A feeling of emptiness filled his thoughts. "What have I done? Why was all this not what I dreamed of?"

When he arrived at home, he took the things into the house. His mother took one look at the unused food in the basket and a change of mood from her son. "Didn't you have your picnic, Jack? I thought this was to be a real celebration before you headed off for cadet training. What happened? Can you talk about it?"

"No, mother. I can't talk about it. What we dream about is sometimes impossible to achieve. I don't want to say any more about it. Just leave me alone." With that Jack went to his room, threw himself across his bed, looking up at the ceiling, and wondering what went wrong. "Tomorrow I leave Baronsville. Carrie will probably never have anything to do with me in the future. I have to go on with my life." Then calling to his mother, "Mom, I'm starving. And I don't want those picnic sandwiches. Can you cook me a couple fried eggs, and some toast?" Jack went quietly to the kitchen where his mother prepared the eggs and toast, resisting the urge of asking more questions of what happened at the picnic.

The meetings with Geoffrey became different. Carrie was less open. Couldn't talk as freely as she had previously with Geoffrey. "Are all boys like Jack?" she thought to herself. "Do I have to be careful even with Geoffrey?" Carrie was quieter. She had little to share with Geoffrey. The thoughts of her experience with Jack was something she could not discuss with anyone. It was something she had to bear alone.

Geoffrey called Carrie to share the exciting news about his relationship with Mr. Brown. When he called Mrs. O'Conner told him that Carrie was unable to talk with anyone just now. "I'm not sure how soon she will want to talk."

"Tell her I have very exciting news about my work with Mr. Brown and the Barbare Shop," Geoffrey said, bubbling over with excitement .

"I'll tell her, Geoffrey. We've not been able to have her share with us. Something very bad must have happened," Mrs. O'Conner answered, with a feeling of anxiety coming through her voice.

Geoffrey was beside himself. He was thinking, "What happened to Carrie? This is not like my Carrie. She's not the girl I knew earlier. Perhaps she will tell me when she is able." Then to Carrie's mother, "Thank you, Mrs. O'Conner. Tell her I care for her very much."

# CHAPTER 18

## *At the Roberts*

Mitch Roberts rushed to the country club on Wednesday morning for eighteen holes with a executive buyer from the A and P Company. His imagination raced forward as he thought about his becoming president of the Supreme Food Products and the possibility of making it a major force nationally. He waited in the club lounge, having changed from his suit into more casual clothes for the game.

Randall Garret, the buyer from offices in New Jersey, was caught up in traffic and didn't arrive until late morning. To pass the time, Mitch ordered a Vodka Tonic from the bar, and impatiently waited for Mr. Garret to appear.

"Good to see you, Mr. Garret. How was your trip?" Mitch said as he greeted his guest, attempting to feel relaxed and cordial, but all the time thinking through what was to happen at his afternoon interview. They grabbed their clubs and headed out to the greens.

"I've been thinking of how Supreme Foods can become a part of the sales of A and P Company sales," he injected even before they began their game.

Randall set his tee in place, mounted the ball on it, lifted his club and drove the ball on the greens of the first hole. "A right smart start there, Mr. Garret. Obviously you do some great golf." A bit of envy began to show. "Can't say that I get to spend much time playing," he said as if to excuse what might become non-competitive, but wanting to convey his passion for the game. He set his tee, place the ball on the tee, raised his club and followed through. With amazement they watched as the ball landed within a couple feet from the first hole."

"Beginners luck," Mitch added, trying to be casual about the play. Then, pressing on, "I've been wondering how we might bring Supreme Food products to the shelves of A and P? How does A and P gain a broad range of food products that keep it on the cutting edge of the food business world?" he continued with eager anticipation. "What would happen if Supreme Foods were to create products and they be sold with an A and P label?"

"A brilliant idea. That could well benefit both our companies,." Mr Garret added. "Very little of that kind of marketing has happened to date. Why don't you draw up a plan of how we might work together, and I'll submit it to our executive offices."

Mitch could hardly contain himself, to get that kind of affirmation for an idea from the level of marketing from someone like Mr. Garret. And that first drive in the golf game!. What a day this is becoming.

The golf game went so well for Mitch. It was perhaps the best game he had had in a long time. Was it the opportunity to work with someone from such a high level as Randall Garret? Is this what happens for one when you get into the big leagues? His mind rushed forward in anticipation of his meeting with Mr. James.

As they came to the eighteenth hole, Mitch looked at his watch. "I can't believe it's two o'clock. What happened to the time? We'd probably best head back to the club house. I'm treating you to lunch. I won't be able to stay. You've been most helpful. More helpful than you'll ever know," he thought to himself, caught up in the excitement. "I'm sorry to be caught in a time crunch. No time for lunch for me today. Since I have a very important meeting with Mr. James, the owner of Supreme Foods. He'll be most interested in the plans we discussed today."

At the club house, Mitch arranged for Mr. Garret's lunch on the Supreme Food's account. He rushed to change back into his Sunday-best suit and to start toward his interview. "I'll get to Mr. James office too soon if I keep going. Anyway I probably need something to calm me down before I go before him. I think I'll drop in at the Athletic Club for a quick one, and get there right on schedule." he said to himself. Mitch parked his car and bounded up the steps to the Athletic Club. His excitement was in full bloom as he parked himself at the bar.

"Wow! What's happening Mr. Robert," Judy asked from her place behind the bar. "Have you come into some great inheritance, or they've invited you to counsel the president?"

"Even better, Judy. My day has been amazingly wonderful. I had one of the best games of golf I think I have ever had," he eagerly confided. "And I had a most productive time with an executive buyer from the A and P Company. Oh, the power of ideas! If my good luck continues the next time we meet you'll be talking with the next president of Supreme Food Products Company. Pour me a couple vodka tonics."

"Have you had any lunch, Mr. Roberts?" asked Judy. "Better not have too many drinks on an empty stomach, if you want to be at your best."

"I'm too excited. Don't think food would sit well just now. Hurry with those drinks, my meeting with Mr. James is shortly after 3:30." He then thoughtfully added, "Vodka won't reveal itself on my breath. I gotta be at my best. I'm beginning to relax. Gotta keep the energy level up. Mr. James won't want to appoint a drunk!" he thought to himself. Mitch downed the second drink, grabbing his coat and hat, he headed for the door.

Getting in his car he made his way to the offices of Supreme Food Products. He parked his car, straightened his tie and ran his comb through his hair as he made his way to Mr. James' office. He put on his best manners as he entered the outer office of the owner of Supreme Food Products.

"Good afternoon, Miss Franks. I trust all is going well for you today?"

"You look most professional today. I'm really impressed with your tie. Oh yes, Mr. James is expecting you. Please go right in," she said in a most business-like tone.

Mitch knocked at the door. "Come in, Mitch. What can I do for you?"

"I saw in the Bloomfield News that Mr. Jordan is retiring. I'm very interested in applying for the position of president of your company."

"Go ahead. I'm listening."

"I've spent a lot of time looking at the marketing of this business. I've made some very significant contacts with advertising people. Many of them do unbelievably slick national ads. They know their way around the business. Also, by reducing the sizes of the packages just a little, we could increase the profit. In no time we could be more than a regional manufacturing company, we could take the nation by storm. I was talking with an official buyer of the A and P Company. I shared my idea of our producing grocery products, but with their label. That's something that no one else has done much of before. We could begin new directions for marketing."

"I'm very aware of how you've used your time," Mr. James countered. "One only has to look at the bills you've submitted for reimbursement to know of your work done on the golf course at the country club or for dinners at the Athletic Club. I'm very grateful for your ideas that may be used at some future date. We must grow the company from the inside out. The company was created around the dreams of my grandmother whose only purpose was to provide the best foods for the people she served. That continues to be our mission. In time, if we continue that dream, we will grow and become all that we can be. But, we must follow that dream. Each dream is realized in its own time.

Heading up a company is more than marketing. There are many people who make this company what it has become. All are equally important. My guess is that many of them have almost no contact with you. I doubt that you have much knowledge of how the company works as a unit.".

"But my dream is to make it what it has the potential of becoming. I could rely on those who create the products to guide us through that work"

"I have chosen my son to be president. He has been fully present with the work here, knows the financial organization, and is deeply involved in the creation of products. He has become very involved with the program at Lily Wong's Cooking School. In fact, they are designing new products that have been created with students at Lily's School. I'm sorry that I have to give you such an answer. I do want you to continue in your role as Vice-President in charge of marketing. Your contribution to sales is significant."

Mitch made no further comment. He simply picked up his brief case, excused himself, and left the building. Mr. James walked him to the door.

The secretary looked up about to bid him good-bye, but, seeing his expression, chose not to say a word to him. "What happened to Mr. Roberts? What's with Mr. Roberts? He seemed so up when he came in, but left without saying a word, or even looking my way? Did something happen during your conference?" the secretary asked.

"Broken dreams are difficult to deal with. I trust he will have time to think all of this through. I hope he will continue to work with us," Mr. James replied.

Mitch never looked up but went straight to his car and drove to the Athletic Club. He entered the building and went directly to the bar. "Pour me a double Scotch on the rocks, Judy. I have to have time to think."

Judy created the drink without comment. Having served many individuals under many different conditions, she knew that Mitch, a regular, was in no mood for light chatter. She set the drink before him. He picked it up and quickly poured it down his throat.

"Another, Judy. I want another" This one was consumed as quickly as the first one. And then he added with the beginning of slurred speech, "'Nother one, Judy."

"Better take it easy, Mitch. Downing them like that isn't good. Are you sure this is what you want and need? Have you had anything to eat?"

"Did ah ask fur your advise? Jes pour anothah. Ah'll let yuh kno wem ah need halp." Against her better judgment, Judy poured one more drink. Mitch dramatically picked up the glass and, with flourish, drank the third double.

Mitch blinked his eyes as if to bring some focus to seeing the room, it being not yet filled with individuals dropping in following their work. He felt the urge to go to the restroom. There hadn't been any time during the afternoon to take care of those needs. As he got up to go, he grabbed the counter at the bar to steady himself. "What'sha done to this damn room? Make it stan' still! Ah hate this damn town. Ah hate ahvery thin'"

Judy called out, "Would someone see that Mr. Roberts gets to the restroom, and see he doesn't hurt himself." One of the customers went over, and taking his arm began to help Mitch.

"Get yuh hands off'n me. I kin tak care of mahself. Wush ah kuld see bettah. Tehyy keep changin' thangs 'round herah." Mitch dropped to his knees. Unable to make his way, the front of his pants was suddenly flushed with urine. It seemed to matter little to him, as he struggled to get up. Unable to make it on his own, two customers, putting their arms under his, lifted him up, and carried him to a booth. He fell over, passing out while on the bench.

Judy, taking charge, "Get his keys. He'll go nowhere in a car in that condition. We have a couple of guest rooms here at the Club. We'll put him to bed here and I'll hold his keys until tomorrow." Judy showed the two men, who had picked him up,.the way to the guest rooms. They carried him to the room, put him on the bed still fully dressed in his best clothes, which he had worn for the interview. They quietly closed the door, leaving Mitch to sleep it off. Judy kept the keys.

That evening, Gladys and Jack waited for Mitch to come home. The dinner hour passed. Mitch did not come. Jack and his mother finally had their supper before retiring to their living room to await Mitch's return. Finally they prepared for bed. "I wonder what's keeping your father. He's never this late. You need a good night's sleep, Jack. Tomorrow's a big day for you. I trust your dad will be here to see you off."

"I hope he hasn't forgotten that I'm leaving early tomorrow morning." With that Jack planted a kiss on his mother's cheek, and went to his room. Sleep did not come easily. Much of the night he thought of how nothing had gone as he had dreamed. Hold on to dreams? Ha! At last he dozed off.

Mother called, "Jack, your breakfast is ready. Scrabbled eggs and bacon. What do you want to drink."

"If'n I'm going to be an air force pilot I can begin to drink like a man. Make that a coffee!" he called down from his up-stair bedroom. He quickly shaved and conducted his usual morning bathroom rituals, and dressed before grabbing his small bag and rushing to breakfast. "I'm gonna miss all your cookin', mom. I wonder what chow will be like in service?" Jack made short use of the food before him. "Good grief, it's almost time for me to get goin'. Dad didn't come home? I hope he's okay. Sorry he's not here so I can say my good-byes. Tell him I'll write and let him know how I'm gettin' along. Mom, I can't wait to get in the cockpit of my heaven-bound buggy and surge upward, up above the clouds. On some very dark, stormy day, when you hear the thunder roar, it won't be the work of lightning. It will be my demanding that the clouds open up and let the sun shine down upon you. Bye, mom."

With that Jack, taking his small bag, reached down to kiss his mother on her forehead. "Bye, mom. Take care. Send me some cookies so's I can remember the smell of your kitchen."

"Bye, Jack. We'll see you after your cadet training." And with that Jack rushed out the door to meet another youth enlisting in the air force.

# CHAPTER 19

## *At the Athletic Club*

It was 10:30 the next morning when Mitch came to. His head throbbed with the full impact of his hangover. He looked at his watch. "Oh, my God, I've missed seeing Jack off to the service. Gladys will feel like killing me. How did I get in this room? What happened?" He glanced at himself in a mirror. "Oh, God. Look at me! I've been sleepin' in my best suit? Where am I? I ain't ever seen this room. I don't remember comin' here." He reached into his pockets. "Where in hell are my car keys? I can't go nowhere without my car keys! "Who has'em?"

It was almost 11:00 when Judy rapped at his bedroom door. "I'll bet you're wonderin' where your keys are? You were so drunk that I had two of the men customers bring you up here to one of our guest rooms. I would not allow you to drive home in the condition you were in, so we took your keys and put you to bed up here. Here are your keys. Would you like a bite to eat before you head for home?"

"Good heavens, no! I'm in so much trouble already, I can't afford to stay any more."

Mitch drove home. He parked his car a little ways from the house. He walked to the house hoping he could get in and to his bedroom before his wife saw him.

Gladys was fully aware of his entry. She stood up from her chair where she had been reading the Bloomfield News. To Mitch, he had not ever remembered her looking so huge and possessive. Her voice rang with disgust. "Mitchell Roberts, where in God's name have you been? Don't you know you missed seeing Jack off to cadet training? And look at you. You're a mess! Have you been sleeping in your best clothes? I've never seen you looking so terrible."

Mitch didn't look up. He had no defense. Lowering his head, he turned away from his wife, and dragged himself to his room. He removed his suit and placed it on the chair to be bundled up and taken to the cleaners. His tie, now crumpled, was hung back on his tie rack. The rest of his clothes were removed to be washed.

After a shower and a shave, Mitch eased himself into his bed and fell asleep. He wasn't sure how long he had been asleep when the telephone rang. "Mitch, this is Randall Garret. Did I have the wrong time for our golf game this morning? I went to the club and waited. I wondered what could have happened. Are you okay?"

"I'm sorry, Mr. Garret. Time got away from me. I don't know how it could have happened," he lied to cover his tracks. "Be sure to call the next time you're in Bloomfield. I know when I'm bettered. Losing a game with a pro like you is a worthy feat." Their conversation came to an end.

"Oh, nuts. How many things can go wrong in one day? What'll I tell Mr. James if he ever asks?"

# CHAPTER 20

## *With Geoffrey and Carrie*

Geoffrey eagerly dressed for the lunch they regularly had together at Alice's Diner. He arrived early with the usual expectations of time with Carrie. He ordered a coke to hold in his hand as he awaited her arrival. The usual time came and passed. Carrie did not come. "It's not like her not to be here. She didn't even call to say she couldn't be here. .I best head for home. Maybe she called to say something had come up." He paid for his coke and left.

Alice noted Geoffrey's concern as he left. "Two people so in love," thought Alice. "We create problems for ourselves as we struggle to understand what's happening. Carrie probably had a good reason for not coming to lunch. In time we'll know what's happened."

Later that afternoon, Geoffrey called Carrie. Mrs. O'Conner answered the phone. "This is the O'Conner home. May I help you?"

"Mrs. O'Conner, this is Geoffrey. Is Carrie there? May I talk with her?"

"She's here but I don't think I can get her to come to the phone. I'll tell her you called and ask her to call you back."

"Is something wrong? Did I do something to make her unhappy? We usually meet for lunch at noon. She didn't show. I'm concerned. Please tell her I really miss her." Geoffrey pleaded.

Geoffrey headed back to the barbershop. Gordon Brown had employed Geoffrey full time, that he might have some time to himself. He was writing the story of his life and the richness of life in Baronsville. Gordon had lived with many of the joys and deep sorrows of the people in the village. Often others had told him he needed to tell the story of his life and the many lessons for living he had gleaned from his relationship with the people. Writing was a lot of work. Not an easy task. It was good for Geoffrey for now he had a steady income. His effectiveness in barbering was becoming much in demand.

Every Saturday afternoon, Geoffrey and Mr Brown.would head for Bloomfield for a late lunch at Lily Wong's Cooking School. They took along a stool and barbering equipment. The students at the school took turns having their hair cut by Mr. Brown or Geoffrey. A germ of an idea for a Barber College in the inner city of Bloomfield was taking shape in Geoffrey's mind. Questions of when, where and how to support such a venture were yet to be thought through. The idea, so fresh in Geoffrey's mind, was not yet ready to be discussed with Mr. Brown.

Geoffrey had a sleepless night. He couldn't get Carrie's absence, nor his ability to talk with her, out of his mind. Something must be terribly wrong. Early the next morning he called the O'Conner's again. "Tell Carrie I'll be waiting for her at Alice's. Breakfast is on me. Thanks, Mrs. O'Conner."

Carrie arrived late. There was little, if any, lightness in her entry. Her face was emotionless; no joy coming from her. She went to the booth where Geoffrey was sitting. She sat in the booth across from Geoffrey. He had gotten up to invite her to sit beside him. The invitation had been recognized, but not accepted. Geoffrey felt an emptiness within himself. He wanted so much to be beside her; to be able to share with her his good news of his work at the barbershop. That did not seem right for the moment. But how does one begin a conversation with the feelings, unknown, yet so transparent.

Geoffrey moved to sit beside Carrie. Instead of moving toward him, as they had experienced so regularly before, Carrie slid slightly away from him. Hoping to get a conversation started, he began," Did you get registered at Bloomfield Community College for the writing class you wanted?"

Without saying a word, Carrie nodded an affirmative reply. "When do classes begin?" he continued, hoping to hear her voice. "Next Tuesday" was all Carrie said.

"Carrie, what's happened? Don't you know how much I care for you? I want the Carrie I have grown to love. As I have said so often,' There is nothing that can come between us.' "

Alice watched from her place by the cash register. She was so aware of a deep, deep pain being experienced by Carrie. Alice was almost never at a loss for words. Sensing the depth of some hurt, but not knowing the cause, she felt helpless, and unable to know how to help. The mood within the Diner was like a balloon, having been full and vibrant, was now without air—a sense of hopelessness seemed everywhere.

Carrie seemingly was nowhere near where they had been. Gone were the feelings of that first kiss on her front porch, nor the times, sitting side by side at Alice's Diner, they shared their dreams. "Some day I will tell you,Geoffrey, but now I can't talk about it. Please don't push me." Carrie excused herself. Geoffrey got up, letting her out, and accompanied her to the door. Realizing the need for her own time, he opened the door and quietly allowed her to leave the restaurant and start her way home. Geoffrey was like a balloon with the air squeezed out. He returned to the booth and almost without taste finished his coke.

Alice motioned to Geoffrey not to pay for the coke. He left with his face turned downward. Alice had never seen him in such a depressed mood.

One week followed another. Little by little Carrie began to trust her relationship with Geoffrey. They sat side by side. Lightness returned to the conversations. Even Alice was once more herself.

It was at breakfast one morning with Geoffrey that Carrie began to feel new things in her body. That morning, as she dressed, she became aware to the sensitivity of her breasts. She also noted that they seemed larger, more full. She went to meet Geoffrey. .at the Diner for their usual time. Geoffrey had not ever had time to share with Carrie that he was becoming a full partner with Mr. Brown at his barbershop. This was to be the morning.

Geoffrey had practiced how he would share his good news. He arrived earlier than usual.

"Well, what's up, young man. May I be present for the good news?" Alice asked.

"Be my guest. This will be a most important day."

Just then Carrie swept into the room and placed herself in the booth beside Geoffrey.

"Three cheese omelets are the gifts of the house this morning," Alice announced.

"Sounds great to me," Geoffrey answered.

Alice brought the omelets, complete with a garnish of fruit on the side. "Just what the doctor ordered."

Carrie took one look at the omelet and smelled the eggs and cheese. "Oh, I can't eat it. I don't feel well. I think I better go home. I may lose everything within me." She got up and raced to the door. "Maybe the fresh air will help." Two omelets were resting on the table as Geoffrey accompanied Carrie to the outside and walked with her to her home.

Mrs. O'conner saw Carrie and Geoffrey walking up the street. Geoffrey seemed to be assisting Carrie. Marty was at the front door as they arrived on the porch.

"I don't feel well, mom. I don't know what's the matter. We ordered omelets but I couldn't eat any of it. Could I go see Dr. Wise? Maybe he can give me something to help me feel better."

"Get in the car. We'll go right now. Thanks Geoffrey. I don't know what we'd do without you!" Geoffrey wanted to go also, but not being invited, turned to return to his home.

"Dr. Bernard Wise" was the sign at the side of his office door. Dr. Wise had been the village doctor for these many years. There had been very few babies that Dr. Wise had not delivered. He was very practiced in his profession. A cancellation made it possible for Marty and Carrie to be admitted. "Now, how can I help you?"

"I haven't felt like myself lately. This morning, Geoffrey Garner and I met at Alice's Diner for breakfast. Alice had just served us the most delicious looking omelet and, suddenly, I couldn't stand the smell of it, and I thought I might lose my 'cookies.'"

Many times before Dr. Wise had known this symptom. He took one look at Carrie's face, and seeing the mask of pregnancy, paused for a moment to think how to break the news, and what examinations might be required to be certain of his first diagnosis. "Have you been involved with any young men?"

Mrs. O'Conner's expression was one of shock. With her eyes wide open, and her mouth drawn tight, she looked at Dr. Wise, trying to anticipate his next words. She was speechless.

"I'm afraid I must ask you to lay on the examination table for what I must do next," Dr. Wise continued, "Do you want to remain, Marty? It will not take long."

Carrie, embarrassed, lay on her back while Dr. Wise conducted his examination. "I must be honest with you, Carrie.

You have every sign of being pregnant. When did this all happen?"

Tears began to flow, as Carrie had to, at last, share what had happened. "Jack Roberts lied to me; told me that a group from our Sunday School Class was going to join us for a picnic, just before he was to leave for training in the Air Force. No one was at the picnic. It was a horrible experience. So terrible I couldn't share it with anyone." Then she told what had happened, with details of every part of the experience. "How could I be pregnant? He never entered my body. All I remember was the terrible sticky mess all over my bottom. I walked home. When I was alone I removed my panties and tried to wipe that stuff off of my body."

"My dear, it only takes one sperm, entering your body, to create a pregnancy. A new life is growing inside you. It is important that you take good care of yourself, for your sake and for the sake of the baby. I'm giving you some hints of things to do and things not to do during your pregnancy. I doubt giving up a lot of alcohol will be a problem! I'd like to see you again in two weeks to be sure everything is going according to schedule Please make an appointment with the nurse in the office on your way out."

Carrie and her mother made the appointment and then headed for home. Not much was said as each tried to understand the information they had just acquired. There was one bit of comfort in that Carrie had, at last, shared the information of what had happened with someone. Now how to tell others what had happened. Ultimately the information will be known. Just seeing how her body would change would reveal the truth. Already, she had noted that her breasts were becoming a bit larger. And, if Dr.

Wise could see something in her facial mask, were others able to see that, too? And what would happen in her relationship with Geoffrey? How would she be able to tell him?

"I don't know how I will tell Geoffrey," Carrie offered as they parked the car at their home. "I care for him so much. He has become so important in my life. How will he respond to this news? But, tell him I must, as difficult as that will be. I must call him as soon as possible."

Carrie went into the house and immediately called Geoffrey who was at the barbershop, "Geoffrey, I must meet with you and share what I've just learned. May we meet at Alice's Diner tomorrow morning? It will not take long."

"I have great news for you, too, dear. I can't wait to see you. At eight?" Geoffrey added.

Carrie hung up the phone, tears welling in her eyes. Her mother went to her and wrapped her arms about her. "We love you, Carrie. We'll be with you through the pregnancy. The child must always know love. When your father comes home we'll arrange for a meeting with the Roberts."

The next morning, shortly before eight, Carrie began her walk to Alice's Diner. As she was near, she could see Geoffrey standing in front of the restaurant, grinning from ear to ear in his excitement of being with Carrie.

Geoffrey had practiced how he would tell Carrie about working full time in Mr. Brown's Barbershop. As she neared, Geoffrey moved toward the door to open it.

"No, Geoffrey, let's stay out here. I have so many great memories in the Diner. What I have to tell you is very difficult for me. I care for you so very much. I don't want to hurt you.".

Geoffrey closed the door and went to Carrie and took her hand in his. "What is the problem? Haven't I told you often enough that nothing can come between us?"

"That's what makes what I have to say so difficult." There was a long pause as Carrie collected her thoughts to find a way of telling him what she had learned. "I guess, to just tell you may be the best and the worst ways. I'm pregnant." Again, there was silence to let the words find their way.

Geoffrey lessened the grip on her hand, and stood unable to speak. After what seemed like an eternity, he said, "Are you sure? How could it have happened?"

"Jack Roberts lied, telling me that a group from the church was having a farewell picnic to see him off to Air Force training. I thought that was a nice idea, if all of you were to be there. He picked me up for the picnic. He drove to a very secluded place. I was uncomfortable with what was beginning to take place. He assured me that all of you would be along. He spread a blanket on the grass and invited me to sit down while we waited for all of you. Then he pushed me down and took advantage of me. I was terrified and walked home alone."

Geoffrey moved closer to comfort her, but she pushed him away.

"I went through a time when I didn't know if I could trust men. Gradually, I built back my trust in you. When I was unable to eat the omelets that morning and you walked me home, we went to see Dr. Wise. He told me the awful truth. Now our relationship must stop. Please give me time to deal with my problem. I must say good-bye. I'm so sorry."

With that Carrie reached out to touch Geoffrey on his arm, as she turned to walk away. She began walking toward her home. As she reached to end of the first block, she turned to look back. Geoffrey stood exactly in the spot where she had left him. At the end of the second block, she once more looked back. Geoffrey had not moved at all. As she continued toward home, she kept looking back. Geoffrey remained where she had left him, as long as she could see him.

# CHAPTER 21

## *At the Roberts' Home*

It was some time before Jack had written to his mom and dad. Gladys shared the letter with Mitch. Their relationship had grown more apart. Many evenings, Mitch did not show up until long after Gladys had gone to bed. She began sleeping in Jack's room. She had stopped creating food for her husband's evening meal. Very little conversation existed. Each day they seemed further apart.

Then came the day when a military officer came to their front door. Gladys rushed to answer the door. She suddenly stopped. The officer look most serious. "Mrs. Roberts, is Mr. Roberts available?

"He hasn't come from work. I don't know when he will return."

"It is with our deepest regret to inform you that your son, Jack, was killed in an automobile accident this past weekend. We are not sure how it happened. As we know more we will inform you. We are here to give you any assistance you may need."

Gladys looked at the officer. She wanted to cry, but no tear would flow. She wanted to reply, but no words came forth. Her body was frozen in grief. "Thank you, sir." was all she could say.

The officer left, and Gladys went to Jack's room. There she counted each of the items that said, "I'm Jacks!":including the little red firetruck, a Christmas present. She reached down to touch it, remembering how he raced it about while screaming a siren sound. She touched the basketballs; and the awards hanging on the wall. She drew his jersey from the Bloomfield High team to her, and the one beside it, the one from Baronsville High. As she held the jerseys close to her chest, the tears began their escape. Gladys Roberts could not fully grasp the full meaning of the visit from the Air Force officer. All she could think of was that she had lost the most valuable person in her life. Dissolved in tears, she cried herself to sleep.

Gordon Brown was at the church when the first news of Jack's death was known. Gordon and Reverend Ryan quickly drove to the Roberts' home. They knocked at the front door. It seemed like a long time before Gladys came to the door. Her eyes were red from crying. Her whole body sagged in despair.

"Oh, Reverend Ryan and Mr. Brown, I'm sorry I'm looking so awful. An officer from the Air Base was here earlier"

"We know. Several members of the church stopped by to express their concern for you. We're here to offer our support for you," Reverend Ryan said, as he put his arms about her to share love and concern. Has Mr. Roberts returned home? What can we do to help you?"

"There is little anyone can do. Jack is gone."

"I'd like to support you with a prayer." Reverend Ryan took her hand as they bowed in prayer.

Gordon reached out to touch her. "Call us if we can be of any help." They stood in silence, aware of the depth of loss being felt by Gladys Roberts. "Please call us if we can be of help."

Mitch returned home late with a copy of the Bloomfield News in his hands. "Oh, Gladys, have you heard? Jack was in an automobile accident. He is dead!"

"An officer from the Air Force was here earlier. He told me what they knew about the accident."

"The paper said there were four young people together, two girls and two guys. Only one girl lives. She was very badly hurt."

Each sat alone. Each grieved alone. Gladys had cried herself out. His lack of contact with his wife only hardened her sense of loss. The chasm between them widened. Gladys went to Jack's room to sleep alone in his bed. Mitch went alone to his bedroom, dressed for bed, and pulled the covers around him as if to protect him from being hurt.

It would be several weeks before the full story of the accident was revealed. The one surviving girl, though now very hurt, would tell the story. "Jack and his cadet buddy got a weekend pass. They hitched a ride into town and went straight to a bar. Because they were servicemen, the bartender supplied drinks. The guys saw we two girls, and probably thought we were an easy catch. They began drinking with us. Then Jack suggested, if we had a car, we might go for a drive. My girlfriend had a spiffy roadster. She held up the keys to show off her gift. Jack grabbed the keys and headed for the car. The four of us popped in the car. Jack, placing the keys in the ignition, started the car, raced the motor to demonstrated its power and in one swift action, took off down the highway. He loved the sense of power he had when he raced the motor. The drinks had resulted in his inability to see clearly. They came to a sharp turn in the road. Being unaware of the roads, we missed the curve, plowed over a bank and struck a tree. It was some time before someone saw the accident and rushed all of us to the hospital. I am the only one to survive. I shall be married to this wheelchair for the rest of my life."

The full story was published in the Bloomfield News. Geoffrey held the paper in his hand, wondering what might be the appropriate action to take. What would happen to Carrie now? Pausing briefly, he laid the paper on the chair where he had been sitting. He picked up the phone and called the O'Conner home. "Hello, Mr. O'Conner. May I come to speak with you about what is on my mind?"

"Why, sure Geoffrey. When would you like to come?"

"Right now, if that's not a problem"

"No problem."

Geoffrey hung up the phone, grabbed his jacket and headed out the door. He almost raced his way to the O'Conner home. He bounded up the steps and knocked at the front door. Craig got up from his chair where he had been reading the account of Jack Roberts' death in the Bloomfield News.

"Come in, Geoffrey. Have a seat on the sofa."

Geoffrey glanced about the room. Marty set aside the knitting she had started, a baby blanket for a crib. Carrie sat quietly in a chair across from the sofa, her expression showed no sign of feeling. Her eyes looked forward, but seemingly without seeing. Her face was frozen like a carved wooden mask, or a shattered glass through which one could not see within.

"I'll come right to my point, Mr. O'Conner. For several days I tried to share with Carrie my good fortune. Gordon Brown has given me a full time job at his barbershop so he could write and explore ideas that he said have been bouncing around in his head. My world was rich and full until Carrie told me about what had happened to her. I thought my life had ended. My words that 'nothing could come between us' seemed empty and meaningless. Today when I read the Bloomfield News and the story of Jack's death, a thought burst forth in my head. Carrie's child must have a father. I would be that father if Carrie will have me as her husband."

With those words, Carrie got up from her chair. The lines on her face softened. Her eyes suddenly acquired a gleam. The mask fell away. The shattered glass was no more. She crossed the room and sat beside Geoffrey, moving her body into the curve of his arm.

Geoffrey continued, "I'm asking your and Mrs. O'Conner's permission, and blessing, to marry your Carrie I have grown to love her more deeply than anything in my life."

Craig and Marty O'Conners looked at each other. They saw a spark of excitement in Carrie's face, and her moving closer to the man of her dreams. As Craig and Marty silently, but loudly, nodded to each other their approval, Craig answered, "You most certainly have our permission and blessing. Young man, you are a blessing."

Geoffrey drew Carrie to himself and. without embarrassment, .planted a kiss on Carrie's lips. "You have made my day!" Geoffrey thought he might explode, being so sure that what had happened was so right. "The choice of the wedding arrangements I leave to you. I would be most pleased if our wedding was a public wedding at our church, where we can declare our love to each other and to all of Baronsville."

Marty left her chair, went to Carrie and Geoffrey and circled her arms about them in an embrace. "Thank you, Geoffrey. You are a very special young man, a wonderful gift of a son. We have much planning to do in the next days and weeks."

Geoffrey lovingly embraced his wife-to-be, and kissed her before bidding his good-byes and heading for home. Not since that first kiss on the O'Conner's front porch had he felt so excited. He headed for home, his feet barely touching the ground.

# CHAPTER 22

## *At the Robert's Home*

Life was not at all joyous at the Roberts. Gladys never knew when Mitch would come home. He never talked about what had kept him so late. They had little to say to each other. Gladys had moved her things into Jack's room, where she could relive those precious moments among his things.

On Friday night, Mitch came home, having stopped at the Athletic Club and having one too many drinks. He reeked of alcohol. Gladys had not yet retired for the evening.

In a slightly slurred speech he began, "The magic has gone out of the marriage. I want out. We'll sell the farm. I'll give you your share. We'll each go our own way." Without another word, he retired to his room. Nothing more was said.

Mitch left the next morning, having packed extra clothes which signaled his leaving. The weather was dark and stormy. Heavy clouds and rain punctuated the day. Gladys' life had suddenly changed. She had lost a son and now a husband. While there had been many empty times in her life, she now had to make her own way.

"I think I'll go talk with Reverend Ryan. I need to have time to think things through," she thought to herself. "I'll call the church to see if he's available to talk with me." She picked up the phone and called the church. Reverend Ryan answered.

"This is the First Congregational Church, Richard Ryan speaking. May I help you?"

"I hope so. This is Gladys Roberts. I need to talk with someone. I know the weather is terrible, but I need help."

"Do come in. I'll clear my schedule to meet with you."

Gladys put on her raincoat, got her umbrella and got in her car to head to the church. The storm raged on, causing the windshield wipers to do their best in keeping it possible to see the road. The rain had stopped for a brief moment when she arrived at the church. She parked the car, remembering the first day at the church, when she and Jack had been introduced to the people of the church. Her husband had never come near the church. No one there would have known who he was, had he walked through the doors. As she closed the door to the pastor's study a loud clap of thunder shook the air.

"Come in, Mrs. Roberts. You know Gordon Brown, the Sunday School teacher for our high school students. He stopped by to discuss some details of the work with the students. He was about to leave."

"Please stay, Gordon. What I have to say will soon be the talk of the town." Gladys paused unsure of where to start the conversation. "My life seems to be falling apart. First my son, Jack, was killed in an accident. Yesterday, his father came home and said 'The magic has gone out of the marriage. He wanted out!' I often wondered if there had ever been any magic in the marriage. Sometimes it was like having two teenagers in the house, only one was over forty." She stopped to collect her thoughts.

Gordon Brown entered the conversation. "I can't remember ever meeting your husband. Sorry about the death of Jack. That was a real blow for all of us. You have our sympathy." He paused for a moment before continuing. "Maturity is more than age. Some men are fearful of losing their youth. I'm not sure what drives your husband."

Reverend Ryan listened, as a very loud clap of thunder shook the building. For a moment the lights flickered and went out leaving all of them in the dark.

Gladys gasped and continued, "The last words of Jack, as he left for his air force training, and his wanting to be a pilot, was, 'Mom, when you hear the thunder roar, it won't be the clouds coming back together from the lightning, but it will be me, in my heaven-bound buggy, demanding the clouds separate to let the sun shine down upon you.' Storms and thunder speak loudly to me. Those words spoke of a sensitivity that I had not heard from Jack before. I sometimes wonder if he had lived, might he have grown into such expressiveness.?"

Her pastor continued, "We cannot change history. We can learn from it. We don't know what tomorrow will require from us.

We have now. Each of us, with what we are dealt, are asked to give the gifts we were given to create a better, more loving world." He thought for a moment before going on. "What would you like to give, with the gifts given to you?"

"Having been a mother, I do know about children. Perhaps that is what I'm being called to do. Thank you, gentlemen, for helping me to know myself. My future is yet to be fully known. You've helped me discover a road map to my future." With that, Gladys Roberts left the study, and made her way back home.

In the days to follow, the Roberts were divorced. Gladys changed her name to her maiden name and became Gladys Smith once more. She returned to the village of her youth, where, upon attending a few college classes, she began working at the village's public library. She most enjoyed story times with young children, starting with the very young and working with older students as each year passed. It was as though she was responding to the her own grandchild, as yet unknown to her.

Mitch Roberts just became an unknown character in the history of Baronsville.

## At the Diner

It was soon after the divorce that the "For Sale" sign was posted at the old Sam Dawson place. On the first Monday morning following the announcement of the sale, the Monday Morning Guys met at the Diner., "I seen the 'For Sale' sign at the old Sam Dawson farm. I hea'rd that the Roberts are gettin' divorced,." one volunteered.

"Is it true that their son got the O'Coner girl knocked up? Now that's new stuff for Baronsville," another added.

"Don't be so damn smug. You were jist lucky. We know how you played around."

"I hear the Garner kid is marrying the girl. When I was in Gordon's Barbershop, he was working full time. I be very impressed with the way he's takin' over. Seems to have his head on right"

"I hear'd he proposed to her knowing she was pregnant. Now that's somethin' Doesn't happen every day."

That is how news, or town gossip, gets spread around. Once it's shared it loses some of its steam. Life goes on without more concern.

"I 'spect we'll all git an invite to the weddin' at the church," Billy Burch volunteered. "The O'Conners bein' so durn religious. 'Speck she'll git to wear a white weddin' gown?'"

"Int'restin' question. I heard she got pregnant and the guy never got in her."

"Immaculate conception?"

"Ah don't reckon could be so! Don't matter to me no how, not as far as I'm concerned. That Garner kid must be somethin' very special, to take on a job like that. But then, when in love, you do the most darnest things."

Alice took in the whole conversation. She had seen Geoffrey and Carrie's relationship come into being. "If those guys could have seen their friendship grow, they'd be even more impressed." For a moment she thought to herself,. "Wouldn't it be special if Lily would cook a special wedding dinner to celebrate their marriage? I think I'll offer that to the O'Conners as my special gift. Gotta find out some dates so we can make the event very special."

# CHAPTER 23

## *"For Better, Or..."*

A date for the wedding was set for three weeks following Geoffrey's visit to ask for her hand in marriage. All of Baronsville was volunteering to make it a very special event for the young couple.

Marty had sewn a special gown for herself for the event. Neighbors paid for Lily Wong to make a magnificent wedding cake, three layers high with a bride and groom set on the top. The ladies of the church planned a huge bowl of punch, purchased beautiful napkins, paper plates, a large dishes of fancy nuts, and cooked the most wonderful tidbits from the best recipes in the village. This was to be one of the best weddings the town had ever seen.

Late June is a glorious time for flowers. The air was perfumed by their presence. Many ladies constructed their own corsages to wear at the wedding. The whole village was a-buzz with anticipation.

The evening before the wedding, all the wedding party, parents of the couple, Richard and Grace Ryan, all came together at Alice's Diner for a special dinner prepared by Lily Wong and offered as a gift to the bride and groom by Alice. Getting live lobsters to a small village like Baronsville is difficult. Alice did her very best and served lobster and prime rib, baked potato, fresh string beans, Lily's homemade rolls, and an elegant mixed green salad, with a special dressing created by Lily. She offered fresh peach pie with peach ice cream, with peaches shipped in from southern Georgia. It was a feast to be remembered.

On the evening of the wedding, almost every one in the village came to the church. The town had never been so well dressed. The beauty parlor was the busiest it had been in years as each woman wanted to make sure her hair was as well cared for as her dress.

The beards on the faces of the men were doubly smooth. Every hair on heads, not yet bald, was in place. Some of the men, who hadn't seen a white shirt and a tie in months, arrived as though they were to be filmed for Esquire Magazine.

The music for the ceremony began with Mrs. Ryan improvising a medley of love songs which a had captured the imagination of the young people. She began with the melody of "All My Love," which prompted those in attendance to sing to themselves, "All my love is for you alone," followed by "All My Tomorrows" and the words, "And all my tomorrows belong to you.":

As the mothers were ushered to their seats at the front of the church, Carrie had invited Sammy Brown to sing "Because.". His rich, baritone voice rang out with feeling and passion befitting of the event. "Because you come to me with accents sweet." Many of the ladies retrieved their handkerchiefs to catch the tears, waiting to erupt, for they were remembering hearing that same song at their own wedding. The song had become a standard for Baronsville weddings.

Everyone looked forward as Reverend Ryan, Geoffrey and Gordon Brown, Geoffrey's best man, entered and took their place at the front of the chancel. Grace Ryan began the wedding march by Wagner. People thought the words, "Here comes the bride," as they stood and faced the procession of Carrie and her father, and her friend, Betty, as they made their way to join the men awaiting their arrival.

Carrie appeared radiant as she looked forward to Geoffrey. Everyone thought his face might erupt, his smile being so totally encompassing. Those, who had previously gone through the marriage vows, tingled with their memories of such a moment. Baronsville had seldom seen such total joy. Many could hardly hear the words spoken, so great their own feelings in remembrance. The people could almost recite the ritual, so often had they encountered it.

They did hear Reverend Ryan say "May I present to the friends and families assembled here, Mr. and Mrs. Geoffrey Garner. Love has once more triumphed." Grace began the recession music as the wedding party made their way to the vestibule, where they greeted the congregation on their way to the basement and the reception.

When the bride and groom ended the receiving line, they made their way to the basement and the reception. Lily's wedding cake was elegant, set on a table surrounded by flowers, and the food prepared for the event. Smiles were abundant as Carrie cut the first piece of cake and held it to Geoffrey's mouth to demonstrate her care for him. He followed with an embrace and a frosting-laced kiss as everyone applauded. Carrie licked her lips as if to say, "More, please!"

Alice had assumed the role of serving all in attendance. The Diner had been closed for the evening, so Lily could assist in the serving. A wise decision, since most of Baronsville was at the church.

Geoffrey moved to the punch bowl, secured a cup of punch, held it to Carrie's lips, as she took one deep sip. This was followed by a wet kiss, planted on the lips of Geoffrey. Geoffrey smacked his lips, loudly,. in appreciation and in imitation of his frosting-laced kiss to Carrie. Those in attendance saw the playfulness of the exchange and everyone laughed upon sharing in the joy of the moment.

They glanced at another table at the side of the room, a table filled with gifts for the bride and groom—gifts that were an expression of joy at the realization of a dream come true. They moved to the table and began to unwrap the gifts. The villagers munched on their cake, the nuts and the tidbits as they "oohed" and "ahed" at each revelation. Craig and Marty said they would take the gifts to their house, it being across the street from the church, and keep them until the couple returned from their wedding trip.

The couple said their thanks to everyone, bid them all goodbye, and excitedly rushed to their car to begin their honeymoon. Several of their friends stood silently and playfully by, as they got into the car. Geoffrey began the motor, put the car in gear, raced the motor to take off. The car just sat there. He got out, and with an expression of disbelief, as if to say, "What do I do now?" looked at his friends a short distance from him. They were standing there, doubled up with laughter, before coming forward with their jacks to lift the car and removed the cement blocks which had suspended it.

When it was once more on solid ground, the whole group joyfully sent them on their way. The evening had been complete.

# CHAPTER 24

## *When in "For Better…"*

Upon return from their trip, Geoffrey returned to barbering and Carrie enrolled in a writing class at the Bloomfield Community College.

It was in the second week of the writing class the students were invited to write a story about the community or neighborhood in which they lived. Carrie struggled, just as she had when she was asked to deliver the salutatorian talk at their high school graduation. "I think I'll write about the good things of Baronsvillre. Maybe it could be of Alice's Diner, which is where I really came to know Geoffrey, and where so much of what happens in our village is talked about.

She wrote: Title—BARONSVILLE BRIEF. A short work could be brief, or a brief could be a statement, often used by lawyers, to make known details of an event.

"This brief is about the richness of Baronsville. There are so many tales to tell.

Alice's Diner is a place filled with magic, or it is something that brings out the magic in so many people of the village. What mysterious forces are at work each Monday  morning   as people of the village come together to share news of the neighborhoods, and   to outline events for the week?

Is it the magic in the foods prepared by Lily Wong, food that delights the pallet and   invites out conversations and relationships; the elegant sweet breads, baked fresh each day, or the coffee rich and hot; always with cups kept filled to their top?.

Is it Alice, herself, that always has the welcome mat out that becomes an invitation to life?.

I know the magic, for it was at Alice's Diner that I found my husband. We were always friends, but over cokes and Lily's latest creation, we found each other. The sharing of the bread and a drink wrought a lifetime of promises. Would that all tables blessed with food or drink lead to invitations and a rich full life.

Thank you, Alice's Diner, for the gift of life you share.

Carrie Garner."

The article was selected, as one of several, to be sent to the Bloomfield News, The public response to hearing good things was noted. Carrie was invited to prepare a column each week. Thus her skill in writing grew.

# CHAPTER 25

## *Summer, Autumn, Spring, and Then....*

Geoffrey and Carrie found a little house not far from the barbershop. Carrie found great joy in making their new home a place of warmth and invitation. Two young people, so in love, could live without most things others thought they had to have in order to survive. Geoffrey soon found himself having to do "fix it" tasks not previously expected. Hammers, screwdrivers, and such things never reached the level of comfort of combs, scissors and clippers. But he soon learned that the mother of creativity is necessity.

Carrie borrowed her mother's sewing machine to make curtains. She experimented with making baby clothes, wondering if the baby would be a boy or girl. She made lists of names for the baby. What names would go with the name Garner.? She would, at times, call her mother or Lily Wong about how to make something that Geoffrey liked. She made lists of grocery items they would need, making sure to keep the cost within their limited budget.

At night, each sitting in their favorite chairs, they would look at each other and laugh at how they had become an "old couple."

Geoffrey and Gordon found time to go the the Bloomfield inner city and conduct barber sessions in a site near Lily's Cooking School. As Lily had done in inviting young people of the community to participate and learn to cook, the Geoffrey-Gordon team began teaching the young people how to barber. Gradually began what was to become the Garner-Brown Barber College.

On March third the telephone at the Barber Shop rang. Carrie's voice was excited. "My water broke. I think you'd better come home." Fortunately, Gordon Brown had stopped in that morning following his breakfast at the Diner. "Gordon, will you finish cutting Billy's hair. I think I'm about to be a father! That was Carrie." With that Geoffrey extracted himself from his barber apron, handing the scissors and comb to Gordon and raced home.

In no time he helped Carrie into the car and they were off to the Bloomfield General Hospital. Geoffrey impatiently waited. He picked up magazines, but couldn't stay focused long enough to read any of them. He would get up from a chair, walk a few steps, and return to another chair. Several times he thought he had to use the bathroom, only to find that was not what he needed. "Is this what father's do while they have to wait? Why does it take so long? What is happening to Carrie? There were a lot of things they never told me before today! Oh, God, I hope everything's coming out okay for Carrie! Now that was a dumb statement. Coming out is what birthing really is. How did the term 'labor' happen? How come we have to learn so much in such a short time and in such a way!" Thoughts raced through his mind as he pranced about, waiting for someone to come out and say that all is fine.

It seemed forever before the doctor came out, carrying the baby by her feet. "You have a beautiful young daughter. She appears to be fine. We'll clean her up and prepare her for your wife. You may go in to see the proud mother." And the doctor and the baby were gone.

Geoffrey had, absently minded, left the things he had brought with him in the waiting room as he made it to the recovery room. He looked down on the sweat-filled face of his wife. Her hair, once carefully dressed, was now in disarray. He looked into the face recovering from the struggle and thought, "Carrie, you are so beautiful." He then said aloud, "We're the parents of a beautiful baby girl. Carrie, my love, you're the giver of a miracle." He leaned over and gently taking her in his arms planted a kiss on her lips. "I'll go ans tell our parents. I'm sure they'll want to know. That will give you some time to relax and recover. The doctor said he'd be bringing the baby to you as soon as she is made ready. I'll return as soon as I can close up the barber shop. Bye, love!" He quickly left the hospital, forgetting all the things he had left in the waiting room. But then, one is only a father one first time. He should be excused for not remembering everything!

Preparing the birth certificate was a problem for a moment. While Carrie had made long lists of possible names, they had not decided on a name for a boy or a girl. The nurse had repeatedly asked for a name. They could not decide. They finally brought it to two names—Cynthia Lee or Debra Kay. "Shall we vote the choice," they said in fun.

In fun, Carrie said, "I guess you'll have to. We can't decide."

The nurses assembled for the momentous event. They huddled in a tight football-like huddle, then erupted with, "We've voted for Debra Kay Garner." And that was how she was named.

Three days later Carrie and the baby were taken home. It was a cold, rainy day. The sun remained hidden all day, yet everything seemed bright and wonderful to these young parents. Grandmother O'Conner's hand-knitted baby blanket was taken to the hospital to keep the baby warm for the trip home.

Geoffrey had everything in place for the new arrivals. The baby bed was taken to the couple's bedroom to accommodate middle of the night feedings. Geoffrey had prepared tea to be made on the arrival. Grandmother Garner baked a special dessert to celebrate the day. All the grandparents were there for the reception. It was more likely that they wanted to be there to hold the newborn.

The Garner family grew in their gifts to others. Carrie continued her Baronsville Brief in the Bloomfield News. Local people followed it with great appreciation. The column was so rich in helping people look for the good in their community that, repeatedly, they would call or visit with Carrie to share the wonderful good taking place in the village. Other villages around Bloomfield began to share their good news.

Three years later, late in June. Carrie, smiling, said to Geoffrey, "June must be a pregnant month. We're going to have another baby!"

On March second their second child was born. "It would have been nice if you could have waited another day!" Geoffrey said in a most playful way. "That way I would have been able to remember both their birthdays!"

"A husband was a choice I made. There are things that decide without my choice. Have you chosen a name, Mr. Smart Guy?"

"My grandfather's name was Bryan. He was a very special person in my life. How about naming him Bryan Craig Garner, bringing both our families together?"

"Bryan Craig Garner it shall be. We won't have to have a committee for this one!" Carrie said with a note of satisfaction.

Life continued, with love in abundance. The kids had their little fights, but always embracing each other when it was over. Once when they really got into a spat, their mother tried to stop it. The two of them turned on their mother and said, "Gosh, mom, can't you tell when we're have a good, friendly fight?"

Grandma and Grandpa O'Conner chose to move to a smaller place, where they didn't have all the work of the property to keep up. Geoffrey and Carrie sold their little house near the barber shop and moved into the O'Conner house, adding another generation to its history. The church across the street remained a place of special interest. Each year added new challenges and opportunities.

Geoffrey began to join the members of the village on the Monday morning get-together at Alice's Diner. Many of the traditions of the village remained the same. However, there were great changes, too. The Sam Dawson place, at the edge of town, was sold to a big developer. The farm was divided into small lots with houses being built to expand the bedroom community for Bloomfield. Billy Burke got excited about the monies available. He sold his farm. While much of the community remained the same, it was changing rapidly.

# CHAPTER 26

## *A Final Thank You*

My name is Carrie O'Conner Garner. I thank you for hearing the story of my life as best I remember it, and as I think things may have happened. I've written in what we call third person, as though someone else were telling my story. I did it with the hope that by getting outside myself, and my feelings, I might better understand the forces that shape our lives.

In the course of events Geoffrey Garner became a most important part of my life, my husband, and encouraged me to become a writer, to follow my dreams. It is because of his love and support that I am able to tell you this story.

Parts of the the story are based on his sharing bits of the locker room talk with the basketball team. Some of that is also my imagination at work based on his stories.

I began my story in October, a time of sensuous beauty and at that time in our lives when our bodies were awakening. We were so alive to the feelings taking place within our bodies, and to an understanding of these new sensations. Those feeling, so intense, were well fixed in my memory.

I'm aware that many in our community, also, were attempting to find an answer to changes that were taking place as new people came to be a part of our 0village. Those events and the causes that created them are still a part of our life today. We seem unable, as a community, to work through problems that face us, to find creative solutions to our difficulties. Even Alice's Diner-time seems inadequate

What started as a time together to share events of the neighborhood at the Diner began to change. Billy Burch, a member of the Monday morning gang, when he found wealth in selling his farm, suddenly wanted to be called Bill, for it seemed more important. When the development in the wooded, cloistered area that I was subjected to and painfully remember, became the William Burch Estates, and. the stream that crossed the area was made into a lake with expensive houses surrounding it. Mr. Burch ceased attending the weekly meetings.

Lily Wong's Cooking School continues to prepare young people in Bloomfield to serve the food industry. Lily herself no longer comes to cook at Alice's Diner. Two of her graduates now come daily to continue the traditions established by Lily. The "Locals" admit it's good but lacks the "touch of Lily." Lily is spending almost full-time managing her Cooking School. It has gained such a reputation that people from many communities, in even neighboring states, come to learn her gifts with food.

Geoffrey has established the Garner-Brown Barber College near Lily's Cooking School. Daily he travels to inner-city

Bloomfield to provide services for the young people there. It has become a full time job, Young people from villages surrounding Bloomfield come to learn their trade at his school.

The Marriott Corporation built a beautiful 5-star hotel at the edge of the Bloomfield Golf Course. We had heard that the restaurant was "out of this world.". It is a bit extravagant but for our eighteenth anniversary it was worth the splurge. It became a part of our family plan. Getting it done was late. Two weeks before Debra's birthday, a letter arrived from the hotel saying that we were to be guests for Debra's birthday dinner on March third. On March first a letter came from the president of Ashland College in Ashland Ohio. The letter contained a sealed nner envelope, with the instructions that it was not to be opened until the close of dinner at the celebration of Debra Kay Garner's eighteenth birthday.

It was a puzzling set of circumstances. How did someone know so many details of an event that all seemed to fit together?

On March third we drove to the country club Marriott hotel, and checked in at their excellent restaurant as we had been instructed to do. Everyone seemed to anticipate our arrival. We were treated with the most elegant service. Water glasses were refreshed almost after every sip. Bryan and Debra had never seen such impressive service.

A waiter brought an elegant tray of fruits and vegetables to tempt our pallets. This was followed by a rich tomato-Florentine bisque soup.

The food was elegant. I had mahi-mahi broiled to perfection and a small service of prime rib. I can't remember exactly what

Geoffrey and the kids had, but they appeared to be in culinary heaven with the choices they made. And the dessert, an amazing fresh key lime pie.

We were almost completing our dinner when the chef and several of his staff came from the kitchen complete in white aprons and chef hats. They came directly to our table.

"We heard the Garners were guests at our restaurant. We trust you enjoyed your meal. When we found out that you were here, we had to come to greet you," the Chef said, removing his tall white hat. "You may remember this head of hair. It was your first haircut and what led ultimately to the creating of the Garner-Brown Barber College. Two of my cousins are students in your school. We are so appreciative of the support you've given Mrs. Wong, and her Cooking School. All of our staff here at the Marriott had their start with Lily Wong. You are the guests of our restaurant." With that they disappeared as quickly as they had appeared.

The family looked at each other, and Carrie reached into her purse and removed the letter which they had received earlier. She read the inscription on the envelope, "For Debra Key Garner on her eighteenth birthday." Carrie handed it across the table to her daughter.

Debra, opening the envelope, began to read, tears welling in her eyes. "I want to share this with you. It is from the president of Ashland College. She began:

"To Debra Kay Garner, It is my pleasure, as the president of Ashland College, where the 'AC'cent is on the Individual', to inform you of a special gift given in your honor. Shortly after your birth, and being given your name, we received a rather large gift to establish a Debra Kay Garner Scholarship Fund. Each year following, we would receive another check, dated March 3 of that year with monies to be added to the scholarship fund. Those monies were invested and, with growth of funds, you have a full scholarship, with enough monies to cover books and supplies, room, and meals. We received the nineteenth contribution and instructions for the sharing of this notice a month ago.

We want to invite you to visit the campus, that we might get to know you. You are a most blessed person to benefit from such a loving person.

Respectfully yours."

Debra couldn't complete the reading for she glanced at her mother, who sat with tears streaming down her cheeks.

"Mother, are you okay? Why are you crying" she asked through her own tear-soaked eyes.

"I know who has given this gift of love. I'm touched by a love, so strong, that it would be continued year after year without the need to experience a love in return. It is a love that grew out of pain of separation, and the need to connect, in love, beyond the pain.

It is time to share with you a very special lady who is your birth grandmother. I need to tell you the story of your being. You are surrounded by love, an unquenchable love."

"I want to meet and know such a person. Can I?."

"May I?"

"Sorry, mom. May we invite her to visit us, or may I go to where she lives?"

"I think you should go to where she is. We don't know where she lives, but perhaps the college can help us. I'll call them to see if we can get her address."

It followed that Debra did go to meet her birth grandmother. It was a wonderful experience for both of them. A bond, the circle of love, was established.

I must get back to sharing what I've observed in the years since my high school days.

The effectiveness of the ministry of Richard Ryan became generally known throughout the state. He was invited to become the minister of a very large church on East Broad Street in Columbus, Ohio. He experienced many challenges and opportunities present in the new call. But it was never explored with the same energy experienced here in Baronsville. What was the difference? Grace's improvisations at the piano were replaced with a magnificent organ that called forth the finest compositions of Bach and other composers of organ music. Did he ever truly find the integrative qualities within a worship service? When does the excellence of music become a concert and when does it speak directly to individuals within a congregation? When were the elements of creativity allowed to speak fully? Were there different expectations of what a minister does, or how he or she thinks; those activities that had developed over years of exploration and practice within a community?

Reverend Ryan passed on a little more than a year ago. Both he and Mrs. Ryan had taken early retirement to spend more time with each other. She had continued with several piano students to keep her earlier dream alive. He was often pleased to substitute as a teacher of English, from time to time. He also found pleasure when a pastor in the area would need to be away, and he was asked to "fill" the pulpit. In the desire to renew the energies once experienced, they had moved back to Baronsville. Richard death in the village was greatly grieved. Now alone, she accepted a few more students, and taught piano students in her home. She continued with her first dream, that of teaching music.

One bright thing did happen. Sammy Brown, so loved by students at the high school., upon his retirement, brought his family to Baronsville. He met every Monday morning at Alice's Diner with the men of the town. His knowledge of so many of us was a topic of conversation that supported integration in our community. Our love for him helped bridge his acceptance in the community, and the beginning of a caring community.

When Grace Ryan moved away, the school board hired an incredible black music teacher. Her ability to connect with the depth of the music made her acceptable to all in town. Everyone loved the music the youth were singing, because it seemed to reach in where people could understand its purpose. It spoke to their souls.

Jack Roberts was killed in an automobile accident before he ever experienced the surge and power connected with his flying. He never knew he had fathered a child, and he never said good-bye to his father when he left for service. Was his impulsiveness a part of his problem? How is it that the normal urges associated with growing up, if left unbridled, become a problem, not only for the perpetrator, but for others as well?

Mr. Roberts, who was rejected for being president of Supreme Food Products, and having lost his son, and a separation in his marriage, sold the Sam Dawson farm for many times what he had paid for it to a developer who subdivided the land on each side of the main highway. Now the farm is part of a major bedroom community for people who wanted to escape the problems of Bloomfield.

That act alone has had a lasting impact on the personal values of the residents of Baronsville. With the influx of many new people, many not becoming a part of the social fabric of the community, the well known, and practiced, code of ethics began to change. Trust levels were noticeably changed. We began to lock our houses and cars. Neighbors no longer met in each others back yards for weekly barbeques and the making of homemade ice cream. Often people moved into the neighborhood and we didn't bother to get to know them. We knew a little about each other, but we didn't know each other. What caused a lack of openness and vulnerability? Did we get so busy doing things that we forgot that our relationship with others were very important? Do things become more important than building a community of support as we once knew it?

Often we look to those who move into our community as the problem. But, did we invite them into what we were about? Is that still a problem with having people come together? What if the invitations were extended to those about us? Are our invitations with those with whom we have much in common genuine, and really done for the empowerment of those being invited?

Lily Wong's Cooking School became the place where everyone in the region chose to go to learn to be a chef. Alice's Diner began to change. The rush of getting things done often limited the time people had to share their thoughts. The Monday morning sessions, a blend of masculine gossip and philosophy, dwindled and seldom had the energy once known. Former students of Lily Wong's Cooking School now served the Diner. Gone was the creativity of finding new combinations of food to tickle the pallet. Alice's age was being realized. The changes with the people coming to her restaurant was no longer as engaging. We now celebrate the memory of what once was. We must search for the potential of now and the future.

The Garner-Brown Barber College, which Geoffrey started in Bloomfield near Lily Wong's Cooking School, flourished. Geoffrey saw how the Cooking School had given purpose to the young people of inner-city Bloomfield. His mentor, Gordon Brown, spent much time in the college helping the young people succeed. A foundation in Bloomfield awarded a rather large grant to the college to recognize the effect it had on bridging the needs of the community with a profession for its youth.

My column, Baronsville's Briefs, in the Bloomfield News, became a regular column shortly after I began my writing classes at the Bloomfield Community College. My practice in writing was helped by the discipline required by publication deadlines. Writing became almost addictive. Every event I heard about became the core of a story. I have several books in process. Each receive my attention as thoughts come to me. There is as much joy in thinking through a story as in having it reach publication.

Much of my thinking, these days, is centered around the topic of power. The quest for power can be damaging to the recipients by its effects, or it can be a means to greater, fuller life. Power can be a means of control, with the beneficiary being the controller. It is often disguised as being beneficial for others, a solution to the problems of society. Such denies individuals the right and necessity of practicing their own critical thinking and creativity. A part of what it is to be human is not nurtured or developed.

Power can be the means to the empowerment of others. It results in the development of a community, a greater oneness of purpose for a group. By the sharing of the gifts each of us were given, when we give them as gifts, we bring about an awareness of each of our needs and our potentials—potentials to be invited out. As I have discovered in the struggles in my life, I have found it is not the great, large tasks that solve problems, but the small, day by day, almost unnoticed things, that matter most. It was Lily Wong's using her day-off to teach young people from the inner city of Bloomfield that developed power for many in her neighborhood. It was the friendly, first-name, greeting of Sammy Brown, that mattered to my classmates in high school. It was the simple recognition of Reverend Ryan of the gifts of Lily Wong and Sammy Brown that brought many of us in Baronsville to an awareness of the power of simple gifts.

Power, used to empower others, results in pro-active responses. It often invites others to be a part of a solution to a problem or to events, and relationships that enhance life.

Power used to control often results in reactive responses. History books are filled with reports of this kind of use of power. Wars are generated by the misuse of power. Wars can be between nations, religions, and even within groups that began with a common purpose.

As a writer, which I think of how to address the issues of power, I find it difficult to get inside the heart, the souls, and minds of individuals to understand what motivates their use of power. As I once wrote, "We will not change the macrocosm problems of the world until we begin to deal with the microcosm problems of those issues within ourselves."

Our struggles cannot be solved by mandates. We create laws to attempt to solve problems, but we forget that laws cannot effect their full purpose without the moral responsibilities of the people. Too often laws are part of a game that individuals try to circumvent.

The gifts for a fuller life are most often realized in one-to-one relationships, when caring for others is paramount, and when we look for, and announce, the goodness in each other.

I can only hope that my musings on some of these issues that fill my thinking may be of interest to you. Since much can be done in one-to-one relationships, I invite you to come visit with me. You have my name. Our phone is in the name of Geoffrey Garner, in the Baronsville telephone directory. I look forward to talking with you, and sharing our quest for a richer experience. We must hold on to dreams. Dreams are how we realize our values for life.

LaVergne, TN USA
15 October 2010
200856LV00002B/19/P